The Case of the Paranoid Patient

Also published in Large Print
from G.K. Hall by Anna Clarke:

Last Seen in London
Cabin 3033
Soon She Must Die
My Search for Ruth

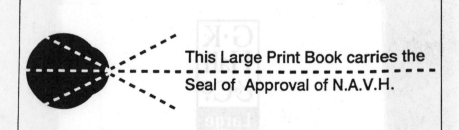

The Case of the Paranoid Patient

Anna Clarke

G.K. Hall & Co.
Thorndike, Maine

Published in Large Print by arrangement with Wendy Lipkind Agency.

G.K. Hall Large Print Book Series.

Typeset in 16 pt. Plantin.

Printed on acid free paper in Great Britain.

Library of Congress Cataloging-in-Publication Data

Clarke, Anna, 1919–
    The case of the paranoid patient / Anna Clarke.
        p. cm.
    ISBN 0-8161-5845-2 (alk. paper : lg. print)
    1. Glenning, Paula (Fictitious character)—Fiction.
    2. Women college teachers—England—Fiction.
    3. English teachers—England—Fiction.   4. Large type
books.   I. Title.
[PR6053.L3248C34   1993]
823'.914—dc20   93-11537
                                                                    CIP

The Case of the Paranoid Patient

CHAPTER ONE

'Oh no, Jack! Please. I don't need it.'

The voice was a woman's. It was very distressed, but the speech was quite clear and it didn't sound like an elderly voice.

Paula heard the words, but they conveyed no message to her drugged consciousness. Her operation had been in the afternoon; now, some hours later, she was in no condition to make sense of what was going on around her in the Windsor Clinic.

Yet something must have registered in her fuddled brain, because sometime later, it might have been minutes, it might have been hours or even days, she heard the voice again and knew that she had heard it before and that it came from not many yards away from her, probably from the room beyond the thin partition wall.

She opened her eyes. The glare seemed intolerable, but in fact the only light in the room was from a well-shaded bedside lamp. Opposite her bed was the window, over which the green and yellow curtains were drawn. So it must be dark, she told herself, pleased to find that she was capable of this elementary piece of deduction, and that meant that it was later than nine o'clock. The last week of July. Two months to regain her strength, and that would mean she should be well enough at the end of September to start her usual teaching schedule at the beginning of the academic year.

Having established this, and having temporarily forgotten about the sounds from the neighbouring room, Paula moved herself cautiously in the bed and decided that, although there must have been a whole herd of cows kicking her in the stomach, she did not, on the whole, feel too bad. At least the anaesthetic had not made her nauseous; neither did she seem to have sunk into a deep depression. It would be nice to tell her colleagues, both female and male, at the Princess Elizabeth College of the University of London, that their gloomy forecasts about the outcome of a hysterectomy had not come true.

On the contrary, she was aware of a great sense of relief and was sure that she was going to feel a great deal better than she had done for the past year.

Sleep overcame her, and lasted until the nurse woke her up to give her a sleeping pill.

'But I *am* asleep,' protested Paula, and had no recollection, the following day, of whether she had swallowed the pill or not.

The green and yellow curtains were drawn back, and through the open window she had a glimpse of grass and a bush of purple buddleia beyond. Tomorrow, thought Paula contentedly, or maybe the day after, I'll be able to get up for a little while and sit in the garden. Meanwhile it was good to rest and know herself cared for.

Conscience pricked a little because she had chosen the comfort and privacy of the Windsor Clinic instead of the big public hospital further down the hill, but self-justification quickly subdued it. Had she waited until eventually summoned to hospital, it would almost certainly have been at the most inconvenient time for her job and for the college. By coming to the Windsor Clinic she had been able to choose her own time.

And to choose her own surgeon. Miss Cecily Twigg, a tall, thin fair woman of about Paula's age, who did not say very much but who had a sensitive, intelligent face and a kind smile. Paula felt full confidence in her.

Miss Twigg would be visiting her patients in the Windsor Clinic today, and Paula was looking forward to this. She was also looking forward to her breakfast. The sensation of having been battered was still very much present, but the overwhelming sleepiness had gone and she was beginning to regain her customary interest in what was going on around her.

She took a drink of orange juice and was

just about to switch on the radio when she heard the moaning. Paula could distinguish no words, but the sounds, though faint, were distressing to hear, and aroused both curiosity and pity.

Paula turned the radio on low and tried to regain her own serenity, but the memory of what she had heard in her drugged half-sleep came back to her and increased her unease.

'Is the patient next door very ill?' she asked the nurse, who was a sturdy dark-haired girl called Louise. She was hoping to do a university degree in psychology; Paula had promised some help and advice, and an introduction to one of her academic colleagues. A little germ of a personal relationship had been established between them in the somewhat too impersonal atmosphere of the clinic.

'It depends what you mean by ill,' replied the girl.

'All in the mind?' hazarded Paula.

'Not entirely,' was the reply. 'It's a case of concussion from a road accident. It wasn't very serious, but it seems to have caused some loss of memory and other signs of mental confusion. Apparently that is the consultant's opinion. Actually I have very little to do with her—Matron seems to have taken over the case herself.'

'The consultant?' said Paula hopefully, but the nurse seemed to feel that she had

4

been indiscreet enough and did not react. 'Aren't the consultants too grand to attend to minor road casualties,' she went on, 'and why is she here and not in hospital?'

'Good questions,' said Louise, putting a thermometer into Paula's mouth. 'The answers are, yes, the consultants are too grand. The house physician would normally attend to her, but in this case one of our visiting surgeons has interested himself in her for some reason or other.'

Paula was longing to ask which one, but dared not remove the thermometer or try to open her mouth.

'Why wasn't she taken to the Casualty Ward at the hospital,' continued Louise. 'Apparently she was—it happened three days ago—but then her brother, who was contacted by the police, arranged for her to be moved here. Apparently she has been here as a part-time nurse, but I don't remember her. I haven't been here very long.'

The thermometer was removed. Paula drew breath to ask further questions, but Louise forestalled her in speech.

'In fact I don't think any of the present staff except Matron remembers her. We've got a terribly high staff turnover, and I don't blame them for not staying.'

Paula resisted the temptation to be diverted into a discussion of the clinic's

5

staffing problems.

'Which one of the consultants decided to take her on as a patient?' she asked.

Louise laughed. 'I'm sure you'll find out some other way, even if I don't tell you, Mrs. Glenning.'

'Paula, please.'

'Okay. Paula. I suspect you're rather good at finding out things.'

'My besetting sin, inquisitiveness. Oh come on, Louise. I'll have a fever again if you don't tell me.'

'It's Mr. Easebourne. I don't think you've actually met him yet, but he'll be coming to see you later this morning.'

'Mr. Easebourne?' Paula recognised the name as one of Miss Cecily Twigg's fellow-surgeons, who worked from the same consulting-rooms. 'But oughtn't I to be seeing Miss Twigg?'

'Unfortunately she isn't well,' said Louise. 'Nothing serious, but she's had to cancel all her engagements for a couple of weeks.'

'So she won't be back until—'

Paula felt overwhelmed by disappointment. She realised that there was nothing in her case that couldn't be dealt with by any of the surgeons, or by the house doctor or even one of the nurses; it was absurd to feel so nervous and insecure because she would probably not be seeing Miss Twigg again while she was actually in

6

the clinic. It seemed that reason and common sense were unable to triumph over post-operational shock and physical weakness.

'There's nothing to worry about,' said Louise kindly. 'You're going on fine. It'll only be a routine visit. And in any case,' she added, seeing that her patient still did not appear totally convinced, 'it was Mr. Easebourne who did your op. Miss Twigg was taken ill early yesterday morning.'

This was a fresh shock to Paula. Though why on earth does it matter who chops you about when you're unconscious, she told herself, so long as they do the job properly.

Her unspoken self-scolding had its effect; she laughed a little and repeated her thought aloud to Louise.

'What's Mr. Easebourne like?' she asked.

'A first-class surgeon,' was the reply. And then, a moment later, in a rather different tone of voice, 'As a human being—well, you'll see. He rather loves himself.'

Paula groaned. 'Not one of those! Is his first name Jack?'

'Yes. How did you know? He doesn't normally use it.'

'I must have heard it when I went to the consulting-room to see Miss Twigg,' replied Paula.

But she knew perfectly well that it was not in the old-fashioned elegance of the Harley

Street waiting-room that she had heard the name, but from the patient in the room next door in the Windsor Clinic.

*   *   *

'Hullo there. Any problems?' said Mr. Easebourne as he came briskly into the room, followed by the matron.

Paula was doing a crossword puzzle.

'Stuck with a clue? Can I help?'

'"Mark Twain."' Paula read out the clue. '"Reports of my" ... something or other of five letters ... "have been greatly exaggerated."'

'Sorry,' said Mr. Easebourne, taking the newspaper that she held out. 'I never read American books, old or new. But one across is necrophobia.'

'Thanks,' said Paula.

Mr. Easebourne continued to study the puzzle. He was a grey-haired man of medium age and medium height, not exceptionally good-looking, but giving an impression of great vitality, of controlled energy, like an athlete at rest. There was also something slightly contemptuous in his manner, as if he were talking to a lesser being than himself, but this, too, was very well contained within an appearance of ease and friendliness.

The matron, a slim, well-preserved middle-aged woman, was looking

8

impatiently at her watch.

'Sorry, Jenny,' said Mr. Easebourne, returning the newspaper to Paula. 'We must get on. No problems here, then?'

'Not unless Mrs. Glenning has anything she would like to ask.'

A cold reserved voice, thought Paula, and remembered that Louise had been rather guarded in her comments on the matron.

'I don't think so,' she said aloud. In fact there were several little matters on which she wanted some advice, but she decided to save them for the more sympathetic ear of the nurse or the house doctor.

'Mrs. Glenning is planning to go to a convalescent home next week,' said the matron, producing a faint smile for Paula's benefit and enlarging it when she turned to the surgeon.

'Very wise,' said Mr. Easebourne. 'It's always better not to go home too soon.'

They stood in the doorway for a moment, looking back at Paula, and she had the impression that their hesitation was due to a slight sense of guilt, as if they had not quite done their professional duty by their patient. But of course I am just a boring piece of routine surgery to them, thought Paula: presumably they would have shown more interest if there had been complications.

But even a piece of routine surgery needs some human comfort and reassurance.

Suddenly Paula was overcome with weakness. The effort of keeping up a bright and nonchalant act, which admittedly nobody had asked her to make, had exhausted her tiny supply of strength. After the matron and the surgeon had left the room, she lay weeping helplessly for a while, but curiosity soon reasserted itself, and she sat up and listened for sounds from next door.

There were none. But surely that room would be the next to be visited?

'What's become of the next-door patient?' she asked Louise when the nurse came in. 'I haven't heard her at all today.'

'She's been over in our annex having X-rays and other tests,' was the reply.

'When is she coming back?'

'I don't know. Maybe later this evening. Would you like to sit up in a chair to have your tea?'

'D'you think I could manage it?'

The next few minutes were exceedingly exhausting. Do babies feel like this, wondered Paula, when they first make use of their back and stomach muscles? The chair was achieved, and she felt as if she had conquered Everest.

'I see what you mean about Mr. Easebourne,' she said when breath had returned. 'Has he got a wife?'

'Not at the moment. The second Mrs. E.

10

was retired last month, but no doubt the third will be produced after a suitable interval.'

'Why does he bother to marry them?'

'He doesn't always. It's only the persistent ones who acquire the title.'

'Do you find him attractive, Louise?'

'No, but I can see that a lot of women do. Shall I pour out your tea?'

Paula accepted gratefully.

'Is your matron aiming to be the third Mrs. E.?'

The nurse laughed. 'She's trying hard, but unless she's got some secret weapon to produce, I don't think she'll succeed. There are other candidates.'

'Younger? Prettier?'

'Not necessarily, but with more money. That's the prime qualification.'

'But surely he can't be short of money,' protested Paula. 'He seems to charge enormous fees.'

'Two ex-wives,' said Louise, sitting down on the end of the bed and helping herself to a biscuit, 'plus two houses to keep up—no, I believe it's three now. There's the Hampstead one, and the country cottage in Wales, and a new little love-nest in Spain.'

'Are all these superior surgeons like that?'

'Many of them.'

'But not the women, surely? They don't acquire all these houses and a string of

11

expensive ex-husbands.'

Louise laughed. 'You'd be surprised.' Then, more seriously, 'There aren't many women who make it to the top. Miss Twigg has aged parents to support, and nieces and nephews who scrounge on her.'

'Ah, she would. That's just what would happen to Miss Twigg. I do wish she wasn't ill. Selfishly, because I was looking forward to seeing her again. There's several things I wanted to ask her.'

'Maybe I can help?'

The conversation became strictly medical, and when Paula's sister came to see her a couple of hours later, there were so many other things to talk about that Mr. Easebourne and the matron and the next-door patient were scarcely mentioned.

CHAPTER TWO

A couple of days later James Goff pushed open the door of Paula's room, leaned over to kiss her, and then collapsed into an armchair. He had arrived at Heathrow Airport barely an hour ago, and looked at this moment in a rather worse state than Paula.

'How was Washington?' she asked.

'Hot.'

'And the congress?'

'Ghastly. The dregs of the world's universities. Apart from Guy Leeming, who must have gone there by mistake because there was nobody else even approaching his status, there wasn't a single original thinker among them.'

'Who else was there?' asked Paula.

She was feeling better every hour, and was beginning to imagine herself back in her normal life. James brought with him into the clinic a great draught of the outside world, and Paula was grateful for it, but at the same time she still felt herself to be very much entrenched in the slow, ordered life of a patient. She listened with interest but a certain degree of detachment to James's account of the first major meeting organised by the recently-formed International Association for Literary Research.

'What are you going to tell Mike?' she asked when James ceased talking. Mike was Head of the Department of English in which they both taught.

'That the whole thing is rubbish. And I felt guilty all the time for not being here when you were being operated on. I called three times from Washington. Did they tell you?'

'No. They're very unreliable about telephone messages, but I knew you would call on the day they did the op. Don't worry, James. I knew you'd never get a chance to call from New York, and in any case I didn't feel up to talking.'

'But you're all right?'

'Absolutely fine, but there's just one thing that's worrying me. Don't look so scared, darling, it's nothing to do with operations. It's something I want to find out before I leave the clinic. About the patient next door.'

James groaned. 'I knew it. Back on the detective trail. You are hopeless, Paula. Can't you even take time off to convalesce?'

'James, this is serious. And I'm going to need your help. I can't tell anybody else.'

'All right then. Tell me. I'm shutting my eyes, but I'm listening. Promise. Cross my heart.'

Paula's narration was rather less crisp and confident than usual, but it was adequate.

'This afternoon,' she concluded, 'I managed to get onto my feet for a few minutes and propped myself outside the door while the surgeon was in there, and I could hear quite a lot of what was said. She sounded very worried, but not in the least bit confused or paranoid, which is apparently what he is trying to make out she is. She said, "Jack—what have you been giving me? It's certainly not just a pain-killer. It's increasing the drowsiness and making me rather muddled. Are you trying to frighten me so that I won't tell anybody about—you know what, or are you aiming at something more

14

drastic?"''

'Paula.' James opened his eyes and stared at her reproachfully. 'You're making this up.'

'Of course I haven't got the exact words,' admitted Paula, 'and she actually mentioned something that sounded like the name of a drug. I didn't catch it, but I'm perfectly sure that I've got the gist of what she was saying.'

'Did you hear him say anything?'

'He wasn't as easy to hear as she was, but I think he said something like, "Do you really think I'd risk my career—after I've gone to such lengths to protect it? And in any case, I do care what becomes of you, you know."'

'That sounds rather more credible,' said James. 'He had an affair with a nurse and ended it and she took it badly and developed persecution mania. Either that, or she's deliberately accusing him in order to get her revenge.'

'Anything is possible,' said Paula, 'and of course I don't know anything about her except that she was in a road accident. But I'm getting to know quite a lot about him by chatting to the nurses and the other patients who sit in the garden, and he sounds an exceptionally vain and greedy and unscrupulous man. They are all wondering why he should spend so much time with a minor accident case, and—'

'But if she used to be nursing here,' interrupted James, 'and used to look after his

15

patients, wouldn't it be natural for him to go and see her when she was brought in with concussion?'

'If it were my Miss Twigg visiting a former nurse, I'd just think it kind of her, but when it's this horrible man who—'

James interrupted again. 'The sooner you get out of here the better. When are you going to the convalescent home?'

'Next week. But James, please listen. And please help. It's really worrying me. I'm sure there's something very nasty going on. I can walk a little bit now as long as I've got something to hold on to, and tonight I'm going next door to talk to this woman Margaret—that's her name, I heard him say it—and try to find out just what it is that she suspects about the drugs. And if I can get hold of some of the tablets she's being given, then I'll want somebody to go and get them analysed, and that's where you come in.'

'Paula!' James was sitting upright now and looking very wide awake. 'You can't do this sort of thing. You can't meddle with the business of the clinic like this. Mr. Jack what's-his-name will refuse to treat you. He'll sue you for slander. They'll turn you out. For heaven's sake leave it alone this time. You're not fit to take on the whole medical establishment.'

'I've meddled with other people's affairs before,' said Paula obstinately, 'and you've

16

helped me with it.'

'I know, but you were in a normal state of health.'

They argued for some time. In the end Paula, feeling suddenly completely exhausted, leaned back against the pillows and said weakly, 'If you won't help, then I'll have to get somebody else. But it'll make it much more risky, having someone I don't really trust.'

James capitulated. 'Talking about blackmail,' he said, 'you're not so bad at it yourself, are you?'

'The weak must use what weapons they can,' said Paula smugly. 'I've got to rest now, James, and save my energies. I'll wait till the night staff have brought round the hot drinks and drugs. Unless one of us rings, they won't come down this end of the corridor after that.'

Some hours later, feeling rather guilty as well as shaky on her legs and somewhat giddy, Paula came out into the corridor and knocked softly on her neighbour's door. Then she leant against the wall with her head near the door and listened closely. There were faint sounds that could have been made by someone moving about, but she was not sure whether these came from behind the door or from further along the passage.

Paula pressed closer. The door began to open from inside, and she very nearly fell

17

forward into the room. A hand gripped her arm and she regained her balance. She took a couple of steps, guided by the supporting grip, and collapsed onto the bed.

'Thanks,' she murmured. 'I'm sorry.'

'Are you all right? Shall I ring for the nurse?'

It had to be the same voice of course, but it was so different from the one that had made those sounds of distress that it was barely recognisable. It was low, unhurried, and reassuring, but with a trace of bossiness present. Its owner sat down on the bed beside Paula and continued, 'I'm glad you've come. I was thinking of coming in to see you. Louise told me you were recovering very well from the op.'

Paula turned to see a woman in a pale blue dressing-gown. Her hair was very dark and her face pale. She looked ill and strained, but there was nothing weak about the face. The brown eyes were alert and regarded Paula with interest and curiosity.

They smiled at each other.

'I've been longing to come and see you,' said Paula. 'I thought you might be'—she hesitated—'having problems. It's not my business, I know, but I've been lying there thinking about you.'

'I've been doing the same. The partition is very thin. And I am certainly having problems. Are you comfortable? Would you

18

rather sit in the chair? I'm going to get back into bed.'

They rearranged themselves.

'Paula Glenning,' said the dark woman. 'I read your book about the women who minister to male literary genius. I've become interested in the private lives of great writers since I married into the literary critic trade myself.'

'Literary critic?'

Paula, who had set out in a mood composed of chivalry and curiosity in almost equal parts, was finding it difficult to adjust to the way things had turned out. It was rather as if they were two people meeting at a social gathering, getting to know each other, finding topics of mutual interest.

'Guy Leeming,' said the dark woman, 'who surely needs no introduction to a teacher of English Literature. We got married not very long ago. He's in Washington at the moment, or rather, he *has* been in Washington but he's now travelling around the States visiting people. That's why I'm in this mess. It wouldn't have happened if Guy had been at home. My name is Margaret. I'm a nurse. I used to work here in the clinic.'

'Yes, I know,' said Paula. 'And of course I know of your husband. I was talking about him to my colleague who has just got back from Washington. He said that Guy's was the only speech worth hearing.'

The two women surveyed each other with satisfaction. Then Margaret said, 'The trouble is that I can't get hold of Guy. He's making arrangements as he goes along, and he was to call me every day, morning and evening, to let me know where—'

'Where was he to call you?' broke in Paula.

'At my brother's. I'm staying there while Guy is away. My sister-in-law died not very long ago and Tony is still very shattered. So is Emma, their only child. She's not quite yet twelve. She was in the back of the car and only had a few bruises, thank heaven.'

'And you?'

'I don't know, Paula. That's what's worrying me. I've got minor bruises all over and I certainly had a bang on the head, but I'm quite sure that I'd have been out and about again by now if it hadn't been for—'

Margaret broke off and pressed her hands to her head.

'It sounds quite crazy, and you'll probably think I'm suffering from delusions following concussion, which is what everyone else thinks.'

Paula waited.

'I'm much better today,' Margaret went on, 'because I haven't swallowed any of the tablets. Jenny—that's the matron—brings them to me, and today I've managed to hold each one under my tongue and spit it out after she'd gone. My cat used to do that when I tried to dose her. Cats are very wise.' She smiled faintly.

'Have you still got them?' asked Paula. 'Could one find out what they are?'

Margaret felt under the pillow and produced a white tissue. 'They are somewhat disintegrated,' she said, 'but a competent chemist ought to be able to identify them. I was going to give them to Emma when Tony brings her tomorrow. She's a bright child and the only person I can trust.'

'Not your brother?'

Margaret began to shake her head, then winced at the movement. 'Tony would never be able to keep it to himself, and he'd never question any authority, medical or otherwise. He's not a strong character. Emma is like her mother, but she's so young, and her mother's death—'

'Perhaps I could get the tablets analysed for you,' suggested Paula.

'How? You can't get out of here. Not yet, at any rate.'

'No, but James can. And he's absolutely trustworthy. He and I couldn't be closer if we'd been married for years. As a matter of fact,' continued Paula in a rush, 'I heard enough through the wall—I'm sorry, but I couldn't help it—to set me wondering and suspecting that there was something very wrong, and the main reason why I came in to

21

see you was to find out if I could help at all.'

'You heard? Yes, I suppose you did. I've heard a bit too. Your James has a nice voice. Rather too upper-class for my taste, but not offensively so.'

Again she smiled at Paula.

'I think I'd better tell you the whole story. Are you getting very tired, or do you feel well enough to sit up?'

'I'm all right, but if somebody comes in—'

'They don't like patients visiting each other, but there's no actual rule against it. Leave it to me if the night nurse appears.'

CHAPTER THREE

'Before I married Guy,' said Margaret in a calm, matter-of-fact manner, 'I'd been having a relationship with Jack Easebourne. My first marriage had broken up and I was very disorientated and very—shall we say?—available. He was looking around for someone available at the time—and also someone cheap—owing to various personal and financial difficulties that he had got into.

'Money, by the way, is the driving force of his life. Sex is subsidiary. Important, but subsidiary, since up till now it has always been more easy to come by than money is. You're looking doubtful, Paula.'

'Well, actually I don't find him at all attractive,' admitted Paula.

'Neither do I now, but at the time—Anyway, there is absolutely nothing that Jack would not do for money.'

'He'd kill for it?'

'I believe so, but I may be wrong. In any case it's probably unprovable, but he's been scared of me ever since it happened, so perhaps he is more at risk than I think. It could, of course, damage his career even if not proved. I've talked it over with Guy and he thinks I ought to come forward with my suspicions, but I've never managed to bring myself to do it. Maybe I'm just cowardly. Maybe, when you have once been very close to somebody ... and of course I could well be wrong.

'You know, Paula, lots of things happen with the nursing of old and confused people that are best not talked about. People think that the questions of right and wrong, euthanasia or not euthanasia, are simple and clear-cut, but they aren't. Especially with modern drugs. A normal dose for one person can be a killer for another.

'The case in point was about three years ago. It was an old man whom I will call Fred. A distant relative of Jack's on whom he had once done a minor operation. Fred was very old and very frail and when the condition started up again there was no question of any further surgery or of anything but to keep him as comfortable as possible.

'He was also very muddled in mind. We used to call it senile dementia, but now it has been promoted to the status of an interesting condition and is called Alzheimer's disease.'

Margaret paused for a moment, and Paula wondered rather anxiously whether she was over-tiring herself. But presently she said, with a faint smile, 'I've a suspicion that his intention with me at the moment is to make it appear as if I am suffering from this very same complaint.'

'But you're not old enough.'

'It does occur in younger people. Let's get back to Fred. I was told that Matron—Jenny—would be giving him his medication, but I was still washing him and answering his bell. He rapidly got worse and he died in his sleep.'

'But what about the doctors? Weren't they involved?'

'There was a very young house doctor looking after Fred. Recently qualified, not very assertive, and certainly not going to argue when one of the top consultants said he was personally attending to the case.'

'Did you talk to the young doctor about your suspicions?'

'He mentioned to me that he hadn't expected Fred to go quite so soon and I agreed. We never said any more. He left

24

soon afterwards to emigrate to New Zealand.'

A host of questions came into Paula's mind. 'What about the matron,' she asked, picking one of the more obvious ones. 'If she was really helping him to hasten on Fred's death, then she's much more of a danger to him than you are.'

'Presumably they had come to some arrangement.'

'But if she wanted to marry him? I mean,' Paula stumbled on, 'I gather that he has married someone else since then and that that marriage is just ending, so if the matron had wanted—'

'She's probably next in line,' said Margaret. 'It would have been too obvious if they'd married right away. No doubt she's been well compensated financially.'

'It all sounds to me quite fantastic,' said Paula, 'but then I don't know anything about the private lives of the top medical establishment.'

'You think I'm suffering from delusions?'

The dark eyes looked at her very steadily in a compelling, almost hypnotic stare.

'No, I believe you,' said Paula, although she was in fact not quite sure that she did. A sceptical little voice deep within was telling her that there was a lot of melodrama in Margaret's manner. She could tell a story well, perhaps even act it well. But that did not necessarily mean that the story was untrue, and the best, certainly the kindest, thing at the moment was to behave as if she believed it.

'May I ask two more questions?' she went on.

'Go ahead.'

'Had you broken off with Jack before the old man died?'

'You mean, had Jack broken off with me. The answer is yes. He'd dispensed with my services a few weeks previously. But by then I'd already met Guy and we were becoming interested in each other. Jack didn't know that. He believed—still believes—that I was a woman scorned and resentful. Even since my marriage. Once in love with him, always in love with him. What's the next question?'

'Financial. I take it that the old man left a lot of money to Jack?'

'He did indeed. It resulted in a fresh wave of house-purchasing.'

'Thanks.' Paula got slowly and unsteadily to her feet. 'Margaret, we're both very tired, and I'm only fit for sleep. I'll see James tomorrow morning and get him to find out about the tablets. What are you going to do? If they really are trying to drug you, won't they be suspicious if you are too lively?'

'I'll put on an act. And I'm hoping, if I keep clear of all medication, to be fit enough to discharge myself in a day or two. I'd have

26

walked out this afternoon, but I knew I wasn't fit. Besides, I want to know what he's up to. If Jack Easebourne is trying to scare me into silence, then I want to know so that I can handle it.'

'But you said this was three years ago. Wouldn't he have tried it before?'

'I'm not sure that he hasn't tried. There have been one or two incidents that I won't go into now. But he has never had such a good opportunity as the present one. If you really could help me over that drug...'

'I'll try,' said Paula, making her way to the door, 'to get the information by tomorrow evening.'

'I don't know how to thank you.'

Paula was becoming more and more exhausted. She clung to the door-handle as she responded. 'Margaret—can't Guy come back and look after you? Would you like James to phone for you if you don't want to make the call from here yourself?'

'Thanks, Paula, but that is the one thing I can trust my brother to do. Guy was expected to arrive in Philadelphia this morning, and Tony has spoken to his friends there.'

'He'll come straight home?'

'I'm sure he will. Tony will have told a very alarming tale. He always makes the worst of things. I hate cutting short Guy's trip, but—'

Margaret yawned, and Paula staggered back to her own bed and fell asleep almost immediately. When James knows he is helping Guy Leeming's wife, was her last waking thought, he won't make any more objections.

This assumption proved correct. James arrived in good time the following morning, was very interested in what Paula had to tell, and promised to return as soon as he had anything to report.

Hardly had Paula begun to recover from the disturbance of James's visit when there was another knock at the door. Louise, who was tidying the bed, opened it, and Paula heard a man's voice, tentative and apologetic.

'I hope I'm not intruding. Is this Mrs. Glenning's room? Would it be possible to have a word with her?'

Paula did not recognise the voice as that of anybody who was likely to visit her. She pulled herself up from her chair and joined the nurse at the door, where she saw a tall thin man with greying hair, sparse at the temples, accompanied by a girl of about twelve years old.

The child was wearing a light-green summer dress. She had hazel eyes and thick brown hair tied with a green ribbon, and she stood very still, watching and listening. Paula had the impression of great isolation, as if there was no connection at all between the child and the man beside her.

'I'm Mrs. Glenning.' Paula looked enquiringly at them both as she spoke.

The man began to fuss, pulling a chair forward, urging Paula to sit down, apologising for intruding, apologising for tiring her. The child watched him. The expression on her face was detached, critical, much too mature for her age.

Paula, obliged to be seated, turned to her. 'Is your name Emma?'

'Yes,' was the brief reply.

'Then it must be your aunt who is next door. I had a talk with her yesterday and she told me about you. And about your father,' she added rather belatedly with a glance at the thin grey man.

'Would you like some coffee?' suggested Louise, standing in the doorway.

'Please,' said Paula. 'And for Mr.—?'

'Fielding,' said the man.

'And Emma?'

'Yes please.'

'Wouldn't you rather have orange juice, darling?' suggested her father.

'No thank you,' was the uncompromising reply.

The nurse departed, and Paula decided to leave it to Margaret's brother to begin. For a moment or two he moved restlessly around the little room, while Emma sat down on the bed and picked up the book that Paula was reading, which happened to be one of the political novels of Anthony Trollope.

'I haven't read this one,' said Emma, 'but I like *Barchester Towers.*'

'Do you? So do I,' said Paula, turning to her.

'Except that Mrs. Proudie is rather exaggerated.'

It might have been one of Paula's students talking.

'Like the Dickens characters,' added the child.

'You don't like Dickens?'

'No. He's too crude.'

Tony Fielding paused in his prowling. 'Mrs. Glenning is a Professor of English Literature,' he said reproachfully to his daughter. 'You mustn't put forward your opinions like that. Her mother used to encourage her,' he added, turning to Paula with an apologetic smile.

'I'd like to have a discussion with Emma about books sometime,' said Paula. 'I really mean that,' she added as she saw the sceptical, almost cynical look on the girl's face. 'I'm going to a convalescent home next week, and after that I'll be coming back to Hampstead. Would you like to come to tea with me?'

She looked straight at Emma, who still looked somewhat distrustful. Tony began to

30

answer for her.

'That's very kind of you, Mrs. Glenning, but I hope you don't feel that—'

'What's your phone number, Emma?' asked Paula, ignoring him.

Emma gave it and Paula made a note.

'I'll call when I get back. You'll be on holiday then, won't you?'

'Yes. Thanks,' said Emma. She picked up the Trollope novel again and appeared to withdraw into it completely.

Paula felt that it was time to placate Emma's father. She found his presence both irritating and disturbing. There seemed to be something unformed about him, as if the forces that create an individual human personality were lacking. Paula reminded herself that he had recently lost his wife, who according to Margaret had been the stronger, defining partner. Presumably he would find another woman to take over the role eventually.

What would that do to Emma?

Paula looked across at the girl as she lay sprawled on the yellow bedspread, propped on one arm, while the other hand held the paperback classic. At least she had her Aunt Margaret to defend her.

Margaret's brother was speaking. 'It was very kind of you to look in on my sister yesterday, though as a matter of fact we have been advised that she ought not to have too

31

many visitors. Her head is too weak to cope with them. Did you find her very confused?'

'Not in the slightest. She seems to be making a good recovery from the concussion.'

'Oh. Do you think so?'

The sense of an undefined personality was greater than ever. Paula waited.

'Perhaps you caught her in a more lucid interval,' went on Tony Fielding. 'Yesterday afternoon she was certainly far from clear-headed. In fact'—and he turned to face Paula and lowered his voice—'I have been given to understand that the condition may persist.'

'What do you mean?' asked Paula bluntly.

She did not turn to look at Emma as she spoke, but she could sense the girl's watchfulness.

'They are afraid the concussion could have lasting effects,' said Tony. 'Apparently it does sometimes.'

'Surely it's much too early to tell,' said Paula. There was now a sort of ghoulish gloom in Tony's manner, and she was having some difficulty in restraining her own indignation.

'Oh yes, of course one has to hope for the best,' he replied, 'and on the whole my sister has enjoyed good health. But these things are very unpredictable. I gather—and this is from the highest medical authority—that

32

cases of Alzheimer's disease have been known to have been set off by an accident such as Margaret's.'

Paula bit back a sharp retort. There was no point in alienating this weak and deeply depressed man, who was plainly acting as a mere mouthpiece for a much stronger character. What sort of hold Jack Easebourne had over him she might find out in time, but meanwhile she might be able to learn, through Tony, something of Jack's intentions.

Alzheimer's disease. Premature senility. Just what Margaret herself had suspected. But surely that could not actually be induced by drugs? Surely the aim could be no more sinister than the discrediting of anything Margaret might say, to spread it around that her memory and her evidence were not to be relied on?

Surely a surgeon in Jack's position would not take the risk of administering the wrong drug to a nurse, even if she was weakened by concussion. Or could it be that he had nothing to do with it, that it was the work of the matron, Mrs. Kennedy?

Tony Fielding was awaiting a response to his alarming suggestion.

'I've no medical knowledge,' said Paula, 'but truly it seems to me highly unlikely that Margaret is developing Alzheimer's disease or anything else. I should have said that she just needed a good rest in order to be perfectly all right again.'

'Do you really think so?' asked Tony.

'I do indeed. I'm sure you've no need to worry.'

Paula was trying to assess Tony's reaction to her remarks, and had momentarily forgotten that there was a third person in the room. Emma's attack on her father came as a shock.

'You're not to say it, it isn't true!'

The child was hitting at him with her fists.

'There's nothing wrong with Auntie Margaret. She's well and strong. You're not to say that!'

Emma's voice rose to a scream. Her father attempted to soothe her.

'It's all lies,' cried Emma. 'She's not ill—she's not going to die!'

'Of course she isn't.' Tony got a grip on the shivering child and held her still. 'Of course she isn't going to die, darling. But she might be a little forgetful. We have to be prepared for that.'

Emma's sobs began to lessen, but she continued to mutter, 'It isn't true, it isn't true.'

To Paula's immense relief, for she was feeling one of the fits of irresistible weakness coming upon her, there was a knock at the door and Louise came in with the coffee.

Emma recovered herself, her father said

34

no more about Margaret, and the visit ended peacefully.

CHAPTER FOUR

'Creozepam,' said James. 'It's a heavy tranquiliser. Normally used only for cases of extreme agitation. Side effects of drowsiness and mental confusion.'

'So it's true,' said Paula softly.

They were sitting in long garden chairs at the sheltered corner of the hedge. The shadows were lengthening and all the other walking patients had gone in.

'Are they safe?' went on Paula. 'I mean, whatever is left of the tablets.'

'Safe as our college labs ever are. All labelled and dated and ready to be produced as evidence if need be. So what are you going to do now?'

'Tell Margaret, of course. As soon as I can.'

'Do you think that's wise? I mean, wouldn't it be better to wait until she's safely out of here? Guy will be back from the States tomorrow and will take her home. If you could hand the whole business over to him—'

'Margaret said she would handle it,' interrupted Paula. 'Perhaps she doesn't want

35

Guy to know.'

James capitulated, grumbling. 'All right then. But I'm sure there's going to be trouble. There always is when you begin to stir things up. It would be much more sensible for Margaret to act silly until Guy comes to take her away. But if she challenges Jack what's-his-name and he finds out that you're the one who's conspiring against him—honestly, love, I'm worried about you. I wish to God I'd never agreed to get involved.'

'They'd never dare to tamper with my medication,' said Paula, more confidently than she felt. 'Shall we go in? I'm getting rather cold.'

Their chairs were now in shadow, but the red brick wall of the building remained in sunshine, the concentrated light on the windows making them look blank and unwelcoming.

'I don't like this place,' said James as they came in through the garden door. 'It's sinister. I wish you were in hospital.'

Paula's room was at the far end of the corridor. As they came near, they saw that the door was open, and James stepped forward to enter the room first.

The bed was made, the room tidied, the vase of sweet peas placed at the centre of the window-sill, but there was no sign of a nurse.

'I could have sworn I heard somebody,'

said James.

'At least they didn't set a booby-trap over the door,' said Paula, sinking down into the armchair.

James was near the bathroom door, looking at it suspiciously. 'There's somebody in there. I'm sure there is.'

'Open it then,' said Paula. 'It doesn't lock.'

He pushed at the door.

'I'm coming,' said a small voice. 'I'm sorry, but I couldn't think of anywhere else to hide.'

'Emma!' Paula half rose from her chair. 'What's happened?'

'They've taken Aunt Margaret away. About twenty minutes ago. She was crying. They said she was asleep, but she was crying.'

Emma looked very near to tears herself. Paula gripped her hand.

'Who took her?' she asked.

'Ambulance men. She was on a stretcher. There was a nurse with them. The boss-nurse. And also'—she gulped—'my Dad. He thought I was following, but I came in here. I saw you in the garden but I didn't dare come out. They'd have seen me from the window. And I didn't dare to write a message for you. They'd have found it. Oh, Paula, what's happening? What are they going to do to her?'

Paula exchanged glances with James. Emma caught their anxiety. 'They couldn't kill her, could they? If she were to die!' Her voice rose and then dropped again, so low that they could barely catch the words. 'My mother died.'

'She's not going to die,' said James very firmly. 'The worst that can happen is that they may try to make it appear that she's lost her memory.'

'She hasn't, she hasn't! Daddy says she has, but I know she hasn't.'

'Of course she hasn't,' said Paula. 'Sit here a minute, Emma, and think hard. Was your Aunt Margaret really only half-awake or was she pretending to be? You know her well. Do you think perhaps she was putting it on?'

Emma sat down on the arm of Paula's chair. She looked very frightened, but was obviously trying hard to control herself, and the effort of concentration seemed to help her.

'I think maybe she was pretending,' she said at last. 'She's very good at it. So was Mummy. They used to have a sort of game, Mummy and Auntie Margaret, trying to see how much they could get the other one to believe. They were so good at it that they'd make you believe anything, and then one of them would begin to laugh. Usually Mummy. Auntie Margaret held out longest.'

Emma stopped talking for a moment, but

looked as if she wanted to say something more.

'I wish I had a brother or a sister,' she said at last. 'Mummy and Auntie Margaret were just like sisters, although of course they were only sisters-in-law.'

There was a brief silence, and then Paula prepared to heave herself out of her chair. 'I think we'd better find your father,' she said. 'Where did you leave him?'

'With the matron.' Emma let go of Paula's hand and moved away a little. 'I suppose he'll be looking for me. I'd better go.'

Her little burst of confidence was over. She sounded quite calm now, an unhappy child, stoical and withdrawn, helpless in the face of the adults' decisions.

'Hi, Emma,' said James. 'Don't look so miserable. We're not deserting you. We're going to do our best to keep track of your aunt and try to help her if she needs it. But we're going to need your help too. Are you a good actress yourself?'

'Not bad,' said Emma, coming to life a little.

'Can you pretend you've never had this talk with us?'

'Of course.' Emma was scornful. 'I never tell Dad anything.'

'Okay.' James suppressed a slight qualm of conscience towards Emma's father. 'Here's my card—home address and college too.

You've already got Paula's, but she won't be back there just yet of course, and it'll probably be easier for you to get in touch with me. Find out where your Aunt Margaret has been taken if you can. I'll try as well, and we'll get in touch with each other. Will you try to find out? Can you do that?'

'I expect so,' said Emma. 'Daddy can't keep anything to himself. He's got to talk to somebody, and nowadays it's usually me.'

Again James felt uncomfortable. Surely children ought to have some sort of comforting illusions about their parents, he said to himself, and glanced at Paula to see if she was feeling the same.

Apparently she wasn't.

'That's fine,' Paula was saying. 'You don't mind spying—well, it's a sort of spying—on your father, do you, Emma?'

'Of course I don't. I do it all the time. But I have to look after him too,' she added in a strained and very adult voice.

'Of course. That's understood. Good luck, Emma.'

'Thanks.' At the door, the child hesitated and turned back again. 'I think they'd better find me in the garden. If they see me coming along this corridor they'll know I've been talking to you.'

'Good idea,' said James rather too heartily as he pushed open the long windows to let her out. 'You don't think Emma's in any sort

40

of danger, do you?' he added anxiously to Paula after he had shut the window again.

'I don't know,' was her slow reply. 'I'm beginning to wonder about that road accident. Who was driving the other car that caused Margaret to swerve and end up with concussion?'

'It wasn't Emma's father? Or the surgeon?'

'No, nor the matron, nor anybody else connected with the clinic, as far as I know.'

Paula's voice sounded very tired, but James had great difficulty in persuading her to rest, and he had to promise again and again that he would not rest himself until he found out what had happened to Margaret Leeming.

'I'm not going to wait to hear from Emma,' he said. 'I'll get on to it straight away. May I take this?' He picked up the copy of Trollope's *The Prime Minister* that still lay on the bedside table.

'Of course. Why do you want it?' asked Paula wearily.

James was examining the book. 'Good. No name on it. Goodbye, darling. Please try to relax. And for heaven's sake don't go accusing anybody of anything. You're too much at their mercy. I don't want to find you've been given an overdose of creozepam or any other noxious substance. Wait until you're in the convalescent home. It's only another couple of days.'

Paula gave her promise, and James departed at last.

A few yards along the corridor he stepped out of the way of a nurse pushing a trolley stacked with alarming-looking instruments, and he asked her the way to the matron's office.

'Turn to the left at the end of the passage, and it's the first door on the right,' replied the nurse.

She was a very pretty girl, dark haired and blue-eyed, and the blue and white uniform suited her well.

'Can one just go and knock,' asked James, 'or does one have to be announced? I'm a bit scared of boss-nurses. They are such very superior beings.'

'I don't think *you* need be scared,' said the girl, surveying him appraisingly. 'She likes men. Particularly prosperous-looking men. Excuse me.'

She manoeuvred the trolley past him. There had been real spite in her voice when she spoke of the matron, but apart from reinforcing his dislike of the clinic, James felt that he had learned nothing from this little encounter.

The door to the matron's office opened as James approached it. A man came out in a great hurry, knocked into James with the black bag he was carrying but did not stop to apologise, pushed violently at the swing doors of the main entrance, and ran down the steps towards a white Mercedes that was parked in the drive.

That's the villain, said James to himself, in a hurry or in a temper or both; and after giving the briefest of knocks, he pushed at the door that the man had left open, and walked straight in.

It was a fair-sized room, furnished more as a lounge than as an office, although there was a desk near the window, and some shelves and a board with notices pinned to it. Standing behind the desk was a woman who turned from the window as James came in, but did not rearrange her face in time to prevent his seeing the expression on it.

Fear and fury, he said to himself: they've been having a row, Matron and the villain surgeon.

'Oh.' He stopped just inside the door. 'I'm so sorry. I didn't realise there was anybody here. I don't think we've met. I've just been visiting Dr. Glenning. My name is James Goff, an old friend and colleague of hers. May I say how much I appreciate the excellent care she is receiving here?'

The woman at the window came round from behind the desk. Good hairdresser and good beauty parlour, thought James, and chooses her clothes well, but it's a hard face, hard and disappointed.

'I believe you have just got back from

43

America,' she said. 'I'm glad you find Dr. Glenning doing well.'

'Very well. Very lively. I was wondering whether you would be arranging any transport for her to the convalescent home she has chosen. If not, then I'll be delighted to drive her myself. It's near Richmond, I believe.'

'That's right. Overlooking the river. A delightful spot. Fresh air and excellent food. The superintendent is a personal friend of mine, and in my opinion she has been very successful in avoiding the rather depressing atmosphere that some such places have.'

'It sounds fine, Matron,' said James, after listening patiently to what sounded like the repetition of an advertising circular.

'Mrs. Kennedy, if you please,' said the matron with a tight little smile. 'We prefer not to use the outmoded terminology here.'

James hastily apologised. He was very good at apologising, as Paula had discovered many years ago, early in their acquaintance, and with those who had not become accustomed to him, it had sometimes a most disarming effect. Mrs. Kennedy's tight smile became broader and more natural.

'It must be a heavy responsibility,' added James, 'looking after a place of this size. I suppose you have staffing difficulties, like everybody else these days.'

'We do indeed. The young ones just don't

want to work nowadays, and heaven knows they get paid enough. When I think of the pittance that we used to have to manage on—'

'But you do have some older and more responsible nurses, I hope,' said James after leaving a long enough pause for her to continue with the theme if she wished.

'Yes, sometimes,' admitted Mrs. Kennedy, 'but they are usually only part-time and they don't stay for long.'

'I believe Mrs. Leeming used to work here,' said James casually, and hurried on without waiting for a reaction. 'It's quite a coincidence, I've been at an academic meeting in Washington where Professor Guy Leeming was the main speaker, and he told me his wife used to be a nurse. I mentioned that Dr. Glenning was in your clinic, and he said that was where Mrs. Leeming had worked. And then I found out that she was here as a patient, actually in the next room to Dr. Glenning, and I intended to call in and see her, but I understand that she has left the clinic.'

James watched Mrs. Kennedy closely during the course of this speech. It seemed to him that there was a marked tensing of the features, but her voice, when she spoke, sounded unsuspicious and not unfriendly.

'Yes, Mrs. Leeming left the clinic this afternoon.'

'She's gone home?'

'No,' she said after a pause. 'She's been moved to another nursing-home. I may add that the removal was against my judgment and against my advice.'

James waited hopefully, looking interested and sympathetic, and was rewarded by a further remark, spoken in a low voice that seemed to be addressed more to herself than to him.

'At any rate it's no longer my responsibility.'

'I wonder,' said James after another suitable pause, 'if you would kindly give me the address of the nursing-home where Mrs. Leeming has been taken? She lent Dr. Glenning a book, and I've promised to return it.'

Mrs. Kennedy appeared to hesitate. Was she regretting what she had said, or had her quarrel with the surgeon gone deep enough to destroy all her loyalty to him? James found it very difficult to wait patiently for her response, and was beginning to consider other ways of finding out the address when she spoke at last.

'It's in Sussex. Not very far from Gatwick Airport. I'll write it down for you.'

'I suppose Professor Leeming has been informed,' said James casually as he watched her write.

'I have no means of contacting Professor

Leeming,' said Mrs. Kennedy stiffly. 'The last I heard was that he will arrive at Gatwick at nine o'clock this evening. Presumably he will then come straight here to see his wife, and I shall have to tell him that she is no longer here.'

James sympathised. She's very angry indeed, he said to himself, and she's also very frightened. Whatever the villain surgeon is up to, it looks as if this lady accomplice has definitely parted company with him.

'Why don't I go and meet Professor Leeming myself?' he said suddenly aloud. 'If I go now I'll have time to get down to Gatwick, and I can take him straight on to'—he glanced at the piece of paper that he was now holding—'to Lark Heath. Then he can see for himself how Mrs. Leeming is, and take any decisions that need taking.'

CHAPTER FIVE

The plane arrived on time, but Professor Guy Leeming was not on it. For a few minutes James wandered about amongst the airport crowds, suffering the angry incredulity of one whose expectations have been frustrated. Three times he saw the rear view of a tall, slightly stooping grey-haired man, and pushed his way forward, only to drop back and swear quietly to himself when the man turned his head.

The sense of anticlimax was intolerable. The fear that Margaret Leeming could be in real danger was even more so. It seemed very plain to James that the surgeon and the matron had quarrelled over what was to be done with Margaret, and that Mrs. Kennedy, while conniving at drug overdoses to disturb the memory and discredit anything Margaret might say, was not prepared to go to further lengths. Presumably the people at the Lark Heath place were even less scrupulous and were willing to do whatever Jack Easebourne asked.

The village was not far from Gatwick Airport. James had occupied some of the waiting time by studying the map, and had more or less memorised the route. He made his way back to the car-park, not yet sure what he was going to do, only knowing that he must do something.

As he came out onto the motorway, it did occur to him that Guy Leeming might be on another flight, having departed from some other centre in the U.S.A. He had only Mrs. Kennedy's information. She could be wrong, or she could be deliberately misleading him. In fact the whole business of the nursing-home in this little village could be an invention, designed to get him out of the way, but it was much too late to trouble about that now. If nothing came of this evening's activities, at least he would have satisfied his own need to be doing something, and Paula would be pleased and grateful.

It had grown quite dark by the time he reached Lark Heath, which consisted of nothing more than a pub at a crossroads and a scatter of houses of which little was visible except brightly-lit driveways leading to equally brightly-lit garage doors. Judging by the state of the parking lot at the pub, most of the inhabitants of the village had brought their cars there, and judging by the condition of the crowd of people in the bar, James decided that they would be lucky if they succeeded in getting themselves and their cars safely home again.

Eventually he found a red-faced elderly man who was moderately sober, and learnt from him that Heath House was about a mile out of the village and that you couldn't miss it because it was surrounded by high beech hedges and the front entrance was floodlit.

'Nut-cases,' said James's informant, tapping his forehead. 'Don't want them running loose around the place. Quite enough of them here already. Eh?' He laughed loudly and drained his glass. 'What's yours?' He made as if to push towards the bar.

'Thanks, but I haven't time to stop.'

James extricated himself, making a mental note to tell Paula that he didn't feel at all attracted to village life in England today. He found Heath House without difficulty, although in fact the hedges were not particularly high and were of privet, not beech, and the 'flood-lighting' consisted of a lamp by the gatepost and another at the front door. From what was visible of the house, it appeared to be a big rambling nineteenth century mansion. The windows were not barred, and there was no evidence of any excessive security measures.

James left the car in the drive and walked up to the door, mentally rehearsing his story.

A woman's voice came through the entry phone.

'Is that Mr. Lambert?'

For a split second James contemplated the possibility of pretending to be Mr. Lambert, who was obviously expected and was presumably a relative of one of the patients, but of course the risk was much too great, and in any case he had prepared himself for quite a different piece of impersonation.

'No,' he replied firmly. 'It's Professor Guy Leeming. I have just this evening flown in from Philadelphia and expected to find my wife in the Windsor Clinic in London, but I've been told she has been transferred to Heath House. I am extremely anxious about her and have driven down here as fast as I could.'

'Oh.' Even through the distortions of the mechanism James could detect a degree of surprise and even embarrassment in the voice. 'Just a moment, Professor Leeming. I will come and let you in.'

James occupied the time of waiting by extracting from his wallet the card that Professor Leeming had given him after one of the meetings in Washington. He had already made a note of the phone number and address of the Leemings for his own use.

The door was opened by an extremely handsome woman of about the same age as Mrs. Kennedy, and not unlike her in build and colouring. But there the resemblance ceased. The matron at the Windsor Clinic was not the sort of woman to attract and keep a man like Jack Easebourne. She was too narrow, too clinging, and when it came to the crunch, probably not ruthless enough.

But perhaps, thought James as he followed the matron of Heath House into a large and pleasant sitting room, it was not conscience that had led Mrs. Kennedy to give him the address, but sheer bitter jealousy and a determination that Jack Easebourne should suffer from transferring both his patient and his affections elsewhere.

He declined the offered seat, produced Guy Leeming's card, and spoke in an anxious and impatient manner which in fact

51

required little acting, since he was by now becoming almost as concerned about Margaret Leeming as her husband might be expected to be.

'I should like to take my wife home immediately. By car if she is fit, and if not, by ambulance. Could you arrange that for me, Mrs.—?'

'Mrs. Rachel Feverel,' said the handsome woman, glancing at Guy Leeming's card before placing it on the table. 'I am very sorry, Professor, that you should have such a distressing homecoming.'

James felt a little surge of relief. At least the impersonation had succeeded: she had no suspicion that he was not Margaret's husband. But she was stalling for time; she would like to get in touch with her fellow-conspirator for advice and instructions. She had been taken unawares and was not quite certain what to do. He must follow up his advantage, and do it quickly.

'Is my wife conscious?' he asked.

'At the moment, I rather hope not. I hope she is sleeping peacefully. I will enquire for you.'

She lifted a phone and pressed a knob. James watched her every movement.

'Is that Nurse Peters?' she said. 'Marie? Rachel here. Could you tell me how Mrs. Leeming is? Is she asleep? ... The usual sedation? ... Very deeply asleep. Yes, that's what is needed. The best treatment in the world, the very best cure.'

James listened intently. Rachel Feverel was putting on a good act, but the underlying anxiety showed through. She was giving hints all the time to the nurse she was talking to.

Very deeply asleep. Sedation.

If Margaret was not totally unconscious already, she very soon would be. This was not a time for keeping up appearances: there wasn't a moment to be lost.

James moved quickly towards the door. 'I've got to see her at once,' he said suddenly and very loudly. 'For God's sake, don't you understand? This is my wife, and I'm worried to death about her.'

The outburst succeeded in its purpose. Rachel Feverel hurried after him out into the hall.

'Please, please, Professor Leeming, I do beg you to talk more quietly. You'll wake the patients. Please come this way. She's on the ground floor. In the East Wing.'

A swing-door opened and shut. At the end of a short, brightly-lit passage another door was pushed open. The room was not unlike the one that Paula was occupying at the Windsor Clinic. Opposite the door was a bed covered by a blue and yellow quilt, and lying in the bed was a woman apparently fast asleep. Her face was very pale and she seemed scarcely to breathe. A nurse was standing at the left of the bed, looking down at something she held in her hand. James had the impression of a hypodermic. He rushed forward, pushing the nurse aside, and dropped down on his knees beside the bed.

'Margaret! Margaret! Oh, what are they doing to you?'

Mingled with his very genuine anxiety was a certain pride in his histrionic powers. It must have sounded a most agonised cry. He laid his hand on the seemingly lifeless fingers of this woman who was a complete stranger to him, and for a moment felt an overwhelming desire to laugh.

The two women behind his back were talking in low voices, putting on an act for his benefit but at the same time conveying meanings to each other.

'You were about to give her an injection?' said Rachel Feverel.

'Yes,' said Nurse Peters. 'She's been rather restless the last hour or two, and in accordance with the consultant's instructions—'

'Restless!' cried James, raising his head and turning to look at them. 'You call this restless? It looks to me as if she's been heavily drugged. Who is this consultant? Who are you? Why is my wife here?'

He had got to his feet again and was

working himself up into a fine state of agitation, but as he spoke he felt movement in the limp hand that he was still holding. He glanced down. The woman in the bed lay as pale and still as before, but there was life in her hand; not just a feeble flicker, but a firm and determined movement. Her fingers clenched, then slackened, then made a slight sideways movement.

There flashed into James's mind a memory from earlier in the day. Emma, Margaret Leeming's niece, talking about her mother and her aunt. They were very good at pretending, both of them, but Auntie Margaret was the best: she always held out the longest.

The fingers moved again. James continued to rage, overriding Rachel Feverel's attempts to speak.

'I received a message in Philadelphia,' he said loudly, 'to the effect that my wife had been injured in a road accident and had been taken to the Windsor Clinic in Hampstead, suffering from concussion. Naturally I flew back as soon as I possibly could, and was extremely surprised and distressed to be told by the matron at the clinic that my wife had been brought here. Why? What treatment can she possibly receive in this remote place that is not available at a clinic in London? Who is in charge of the case?'

James glared at the two nurses. The hand

55

that he was still holding made a slight movement that he chose to regard as approval and encouragement. There was no doubt now in his mind that Margaret Leeming was conscious but was pretending not to be, and that he had managed to convey to her his own position and intentions. Perhaps she had even guessed who he was: Paula would have talked to her about him.

Nurse Peters, he noticed, a rather nervous-looking middle-aged woman, was definitely becoming worried by his tirade. She had put the hypodermic back into its container and was standing a couple of feet away from Rachel Feverel.

She's scared of her, thought James, but she's even more scared of me at the moment.

'My instructions,' Mrs. Feverel was saying very coldly, 'came from Mrs. Kennedy at the Windsor Clinic. I am following them out exactly. If you have any complaints as to the treatment your wife is receiving, they should be addressed to her.'

James ignored her and turned to the other woman.

'Would you help me, please, nurse?' he said, dropping all the hysteria and putting on his most appealing manner. 'I am going to take my wife home immediately and call in her own doctor. It's only a short drive. We live not far from here. I shall get him to come

56

and see her straight away and will take his advice.'

He turned to Rachel. 'And if I find there has been anything—shall we say unprofessional?—in the treatment my wife has been receiving, I shall take action straight away. Will you please help me, nurse? I should like her to be dressed and wrapped up ready for travel. My car is at the door.'

The hand within his stirred again. Gratitude? Or some sort of warning. James could not tell. He had chosen his course, and must continue on it. He leant over the bed. 'It's all right, my love, we're going home. You'll be much better when you get home.'

His face was near to hers. He saw the eyes open slowly. Brown eyes, warm and alive and full of intelligence. The left eyelid moved very slightly in a ghost of a wink before both eyes closed again.

James experienced a rush of triumph. He'd done well; they were going to win. Half of his mind was busy telling the tale to Paula; the other half was very much in the present, keeping guard over Margaret and the nurses.

Rachel Feverel, beautiful as ever, icily disapproving, made no attempt to retain her patient. Nurse Peters, very nervous, very apologetic, found a dressing-gown and then a rug to wrap round Margaret.

'I don't know what has happened to her clothes,' she kept saying. 'I really don't know what can have happened to her clothes.'

'Never mind. Where's her purse? She must have had a handbag with her.'

James was thinking about their arrival at the Leemings' house; they were going to need the key.

'Oh dear.' Nurse Peters became even more agitated. 'Did you take her handbag, Mrs. Feverel?'

'Certainly not. It ought to be in the locker. Unless you have mislaid it yourself, Nurse.' She turned to James. 'I assure you, Professor Leeming, that we take every care of patients' valuables here. It is particularly important in the case of confused patients, as no doubt you will appreciate.'

There was spite in her voice; it was the first sign of emotion that she had shown. 'I am going to my office,' she added, 'and shall be there if you wish to see me before you go. You realise, of course, that we can accept no responsibility whatever for any worsening in your wife's condition that may result from this most unorthodox discharge.'

'Sure. I realise that,' said James confidently. 'And I'm quite sure there will be no worsening. Margaret.' He bent over the bed. 'Margaret—can you hear me? Wake up, love. Try to wake up. Can you remember what happened to your handbag?'

She seemed to be about to speak, and he bent his head to listen.

'Pocket.'

'Pocket?' he repeated. 'Oh yes. Your dressing-gown pocket.'

It was a heavy quilted dressing-gown, with large pockets secured by zip fasteners. In one of them James found the purse, a purse in the English, not the American, sense, a small leather container that held a small amount of money, a credit card, and two keys.

James extracted it and put it in his jacket pocket. 'Don't trouble to look any further,' he said to Nurse Peters, who was opening and shutting drawers in an agitated manner. 'I've no doubt the missing things will turn up in due course. Mrs. Feverel has our address and phone number, and I expect she will let me know when they come to light. Ah, thank you. That will be a help.'

The nurse had produced a wheelchair, and he lifted Margaret into it. She seemed to be rather a dead weight, but there was no doubt in his mind that she was fully conscious and very much aware of what was happening.

'Thank you,' he said again as the nurse held the doors open.

In the front hall she glanced at the closed door of Rachel Feverel's office and looked at James enquiringly. He shook his head and held a finger to his lips. Nurse Peters smiled faintly and opened the front door for him to push the wheelchair through.

When they had reached the car, Nurse

Peters said, as if she had suddenly made up her mind about something, 'Professor Leeming—I'm anxious about your wife. I truly am. Would you like me to come with you? You may have difficulty in finding a nurse to come in as late as this, and your wife needs care. I'll be very happy to stay with her tonight.'

And you'll be very happy to get away from your boss, thought James, and to be right out of the way when the guy who's masterminding this whole set-up gets to hear what's happened.

For a moment or two he was tempted to agree to the suggestion. He had, after all, taken on a heavy responsibility in forcibly removing a patient from a nursing-home, when he had no idea how to look after her and knew nothing about the place he was taking her to.

It was this last thought that decided him to refuse the nurse's offer and to wonder why he had even for one second considered the possibility. For how could he possibly keep up the pretence of being Professor Guy Leeming when he was in that eminent scholar's own home? He had been remarkably successful so far, but for all he knew, Rachel Feverel was already beginning to suspect, and was probably already on the phone to the matron at the Windsor Clinic and no doubt to Margaret's brother as well.

The impersonation could not hold much longer: he must get Margaret away at once.

'Thanks,' he said to Nurse Peters as they were settling his 'wife' in the back of the car, 'but there's no need to come. We'll be all right now.'

'Then can you give me a lift to the village?' begged the nurse. 'My daughter lives there.'

'Okay. Jump in.'

The car was in motion before she had even closed the door.

James's elation was beginning to subside, and apprehension was taking its place. He hadn't any doubt that he had rescued the woman in the back of the car from a very disagreeable and possibly even a dangerous situation, and that he had done exactly what Paula would have wanted him to, but to anybody who didn't know the background to the affair, his own actions would appear questionable, to say the least.

Impersonation and abduction. That was what they amounted to. Both of them criminal offences. This was a very sobering thought, and the sooner he got Margaret Leeming home and into a fit state to take over her own fate, the better.

CHAPTER SIX

After James had left her, Paula lay back in bed very exhausted. When Louise came in with the supper-tray she was almost asleep. A delicious onion soup—for the clinic had an excellent cook—reawakened her interest, and after the nurse had gone she remained for a little while luxuriating in the sense of being well cared for.

It was impossible to put Margaret Leeming completely out of her mind, but for a little while she managed to persuade herself that she was taking James's advice to leave it all to him, concentrate on getting well, and refrain from any words or actions that could arouse suspicion.

She was enjoying her meal and looking out dreamily at the line of the hedge and the shrubs against the evening sky, when she became aware of the tapping at the window. At first she thought it must be the wind blowing a branch across the glass, but there was hardly any wind today, and in any case this was a very deliberate sound, and the longer it continued, the louder was the note of urgency that it contained.

Paula pushed the bed-table aside, got out of bed, and moved to the window, resting after the effort by leaning on the sill.

The tapping stopped, but somebody spoke her name. She turned her head slightly.

'Emma! I thought you'd gone home long ago.'

'I had. I've come back. Daddy doesn't know.'

Paula opened the long window. 'How did you get here?'

'There's a gap in the hedge into the next-door garden. You can get in and out without anybody in the clinic seeing you.'

'And what about the people who live next door?'

'It's not much of a risk. Paula—I can't stay long. Dad thinks I'm with my friend Jasmine. She lives in the basement flat underneath us. It's only a few minutes' walk from here. I've only come to warn you.'

'To warn me?'

The words had an ominous ring. Paula, feeling weaker than ever, crawled back into bed. Its firmness comforted her and gave her strength. 'What are you warning me about?' she asked.

'Mr. Easebourne phoned Daddy,' said Emma, sitting down on the edge of the bed. 'They're sort of friends, you know. Daddy looks after his accounts and saves him paying much tax and that sort of thing.'

A doubtful accountant, thought Paula: that makes sense.

'I listened on the extension,' went on

63

Emma. 'I don't think they heard the click when I picked up the phone. They were both very excited, talking very quickly. Mr. Easebourne said something about Jenny refusing to play any longer and they might have to change the plan because it was too risky. And then he asked Dad about you. That woman next door, he said. He must have meant you, Paula, don't you think?'

Paula agreed, feeling more glad than ever of the support of the pillows. 'Go on, Emma. What did your father say?'

'He said—I'm sorry, Paula—he said you seemed an interfering bitch but he didn't think you really knew anything, and he didn't think Margaret—that's my aunt— would talk to a stranger about anything really important. And then he got all weak and whining—Dad does that sometimes, you know, and I feel sorry for him but it makes me so embarrassed—and said how much he cared for his sister and he couldn't bear to see any real harm come to her although of course he fully realised that they couldn't take any risks and if she ever did start trying to put two and two together, then it would be much the best if everybody thought her memory was unreliable because of the concussion after the accident.'

Emma stopped for breath.

'I don't really think they mean to do anything to you,' she went on, 'but I thought

64

I'd better tell you about it so that you can be very careful.'

Paula felt relieved, but not completely reassured.

'Your aunt did tell me something,' she said, 'but it happened some years ago.'

'Years ago,' echoed Emma. 'No, it wasn't as long as that.'

Paula expected her to go on talking, but the child said no more. She had been speaking in an agitated manner, but now it was as if a veil had come down over her face. She knows something, thought Paula, but she's not going to tell me, whether for her own sake or her father's sake or for mine.

'Emma,' she said, mentally raging against her own helplessness and longing to comfort the girl, 'don't talk anymore if you'd rather not. I'll be very careful and keep very quiet. Although I can't help wondering about your accident—whether it could have been caused on purpose.'

'It was at the crossroads,' said Emma, frowning. 'The other driver was coming across on the red light. Auntie swerved but she couldn't avoid a collision. I told the police this and so did two other witnesses. It was the other driver's fault.'

'Do you know who the other driver was?'

Emma made no reply.

'I think you'd better get back to your friend Jasmine,' said Paula firmly. 'Could

65

you stay with her for a while and not go home?'

'Her mother did ask me,' replied Emma slowly. 'There's just the two of them. I spend a lot of time there. Her mother teaches in a primary school. They haven't got much money.'

'Would you like to stay with them?'

'Maybe it would be best.'

Emma got off the bed. She looked tired and dejected and older than her years.

'I don't know what Dad will do if I'm not at home with him,' she added unhappily.

Paula could think of nothing to say to this. She was feeling so very weary herself that she could hardly keep her eyes open. It had been insane to get involved in other people's affairs when she herself was in such a weak and vulnerable state and would continue to be so for some time to come.

'But I will go and stay with Jasmine if you think it best,' said Emma. 'Here's their phone number. And I never told you who was driving the car that hit Auntie Margaret and me. It was a man who works in Daddy's office. His name's Christopher Peach. He's not very old and he thinks he knows everything. Dad likes him but I don't. Goodbye, Paula. Don't forget to lock the window after me.'

'Good night, Emma.' Paula roused herself. 'And do take care.'

She watched the girl turn to the right and disappear into the shadows. Then she waited for ten minutes, hoping all the time that the nurse would not come in, before she dialled the number that Emma had given her.

Emma answered the call herself. 'I knew it'd be you. Don't worry, Paula. I'm all right. Truly I am. I feel quite at home here and I can still keep an eye on Dad. He's up on the ground floor. I can watch the front doorsteps and see him go in and out.'

Emma's voice sounded unnaturally bright. Somebody could be listening, thought Paula, and made a suitably guarded reply. She pushed aside the phone, dragged herself out of bed and across the room to lock the window, drew the curtains across, and then found herself, exhausted though she was, too restless to get back into bed.

She sank down into the armchair, her mind a turmoil of questions, her body in almost as great discomfort as when she first recovered consciousness after the operation. 'I feel awful, Louise,' she said when the nurse arrived. 'I can't stop thinking about the woman next door. I looked in to see her and found she'd gone. Is she better? Or is she worse?'

'Mr. Fielding wanted her to be moved to another nursing-home,' replied Louise, helping Paula back into bed. 'At least that's what Matron told me. She's in a filthy temper, by the way, so if she comes to see you, I'd strongly advise you not to mention Mrs. Leeming. Why don't you call her brother and find out how she is? He's acting as next-of-kin until her husband gets back.'

'I suppose I could do that. Although I hardly know him.'

'It's up to you.' Louise didn't seem to be in the best of moods herself. No doubt the Matron's ill temper was affecting all the staff. 'I can find you his number if you haven't got it.'

'I've got it somewhere,' said Paula. 'He told me when we were having coffee this morning. Was it only this morning? It feels like days ago.'

'Then the sooner you take your sleeping pill, the better.'

'I will after I've made the call.'

Louise produced a thermometer and very little more was said, but in any case, decided Paula, this was not a good moment to ask questions about Margaret Leeming's accident and her first hours at the Windsor Clinic. Emma must surely know more than she had said. She had clammed up quickly when Paula had referred to 'something that had happened some years ago.' So if, as Emma had said, it was more recent than that, Margaret's danger could not arise from her knowledge that an elderly relative of Jack's had been helped to die too soon.

So it was something more recent, and Emma knew, or suspected, what it could be.

Margaret herself had said nothing about it when talking to Paula. Was this intentional, or did she not realise the implications of whatever it was that had occurred?

How would it be, Paula wondered, if one had minor concussion? One might be conscious, perhaps, but dizzy and confused. Shocked. Not very observant, not very rational.

What happened when an emergency case was brought into the Windsor Clinic? Presumably there would be a full medical examination, then X-rays, other tests, an operation if necessary.

X-rays. These were taken in the east wing of the building, near to the operating theatre. Margaret would have been wheeled along, in a chair or on a trolley, and being a former member of staff, she would have been familiar with her surroundings. So even in her shocked and weak condition she might well have noticed something.

But what? Here Paula's imagination failed. It was useless to speculate further, and in any case she didn't really want to know what it was that Margaret knew, not until she herself was safely out of the Windsor Clinic.

She found Tony Fielding's number and picked up the phone. Surely there could be no harm in asking how his sister was. That

69

was all she was going to say.

His voice sounded very strained. Before she had time to enquire, he said, 'Dr. Glenning, I'm glad you called. Have you got Emma with you?'

'Emma? No. She's not here. Why should you think she might be?'

'Because she seemed to take to you and I wondered—you see, she's not at home and it's getting late. I'm worried about her. Unfortunately I do have to leave her alone rather a lot and she's very sensible, but all the same...'

Paula did not find his meanderings very convincing. I'm perfectly sure that he knows Emma is safe with her friends in the basement flat, she thought; he only wants to find out whether Emma came back to see me. He can't get anything out of Emma herself, but he suspects she has been talking to someone.

'I'm sorry I can't help you,' she said. 'Actually I called to ask how your sister is. I gather she's been transferred to another nursing home. I do hope that means she's on the mend.'

'Oh yes. She's doing well. There's no further need for all the hospital facilities of the clinic, and they need the room for another patient.'

'Where has she gone? I'd like to send her a get-well message.'

70

'It's a place down in Sussex. But she'll be back home soon. I'll give you her home address, shall I? Or you could send it to me here. You've got my card, haven't you?'

'Yes thanks.' Paula thought for a moment. This conversation seemed to be getting nowhere, and she began to be sorry she had ever made the call. Tony Fielding was giving nothing away; his anxious wordiness was only a cover-up for a shrewdly-working intelligence.

'I think I'd better send to her home address,' she went on. 'After all, her husband is coming back from the States tonight, isn't he? I suppose he'll be fetching her home as soon as she's well enough.'

'That's right. Actually I've been trying to get hold of him to save him the trouble of coming in to London. He doesn't know she's moved, you see. And I thought he might perhaps be coming on a later flight and I could speak to him before he left, but unfortunately I was too late.'

The speech went on for so long that Paula very nearly fell asleep with the telephone in her hand. If he really was desperately anxious about his daughter, she thought, he'd have rung off at once so that he could go on enquiring about her.

She roused herself when Tony seemed to be heading for a short silence.

'So Professor Leeming will be coming

71

straight here to the Windsor Clinic expecting to find his wife?'

'Yes. Isn't that rotten for him? Of course I'm trying to page him at Gatwick, but you can't imagine what trouble...'

He was off again.

Paula managed to cut off at last.

An unknown face above a pale blue uniform appeared round the door, and a high-pitched voice said brightly, 'Good evening.'

'Hullo,' said Paula feebly. 'I don't know you, do I?'

'No. I'm Sister Fairfax from the agency. Matron was supposed to be on duty tonight, but she's been called away on some private business and I'm here instead. Here are your tablets and your Ovaltine.'

Paula detested milky malt drinks and had up till now been brought a cup of tea instead, but she felt so exhausted that she couldn't be bothered to explain. There was no need to drink it: she could swallow the tablets with some water.

They were in a small plastic container. The pink capsule was the antibiotic and the little white tablet was the sleeping pill. They arrived every evening and Paula was quite resigned to taking them.

'Thanks,' she said wearily to the agency nurse. 'Could you pour me a little water, please?'

Sister Fairfax did this, then tipped the medicines out of the container and handed them to Paula, watched her swallow, and then said, 'Good night, sleep tight,' and left the room.

Paula switched off the bedside lamp but did not, as on previous nights, fall almost instantly asleep. I must be overtired, she thought; or perhaps the drug's beginning to lose its effect. Drug, drug ... Among her drowsy thoughts a very recent memory stirred. Hadn't she swallowed a drug? Hadn't the other nurse brought it? The more she tried to remember, the less was she able to. The answer drifted further and further away, down long passages, across deep lakes, up steep hills, always out of reach.

CHAPTER SEVEN

'It sounds so unlikely that it just has to be true,' said James.

He was sitting opposite Margaret Leeming in the long low living-room of a three-hundred-year-old converted farm-house, full of oak beams, books, comfortable chairs, and sheepskin rugs. In winter we would have a huge log fire, he thought, picturing just such a room for Paula and himself when eventually they made a permanent home together, but he knew that it was a dream, because Paula would never leave London.

Margaret, in contrast, fitted into her surroundings perfectly.

'It must be true,' she said. 'Can you think of any other explanation?'

She had changed into black trousers and a pale grey shirt as soon as they arrived, and looked casually elegant. China tea was produced for James, and she herself was drinking her third cup of coffee.

'At the moment I can't think of any other explanation for their behaviour,' admitted James. 'But it does seem absurd that you should be treated like this because they think you know something that you don't even know that you know.' He began to laugh. 'It's like one of those brain-teasers for first-year philosophy students—"How do you know that you know nothing?"'

Margaret answered quite seriously. 'I cannot remember seeing or hearing anything at all after I was brought into the clinic that might incommode Jack in any way. In the past, as I told Paula, there has been more than one doubtful incident, and once or twice I have wondered whether he was contemplating some means of silencing me. In fact I began to suspect myself of becoming paranoid about it.'

James interrupted. 'These last few days

74

have got nothing to do with paranoia. There's been a very deliberate plan to keep you drugged and confused with the hope of permanently damaging your memory.'

'That's true. They are treating it as very urgent. So it must be something really vital, really dangerous for them.'

'Would you like to go over it all again? From the accident onwards. Or are you too tired?'

'I'm tired, and I'll go on being tired until I've got these damned drugs out of my system, but I would rather like—'

She broke off as the telephone rang.

'Shall I get it?' asked James.

'It might be the police.' Margaret smiled and stretched out her hand for the phone.

James put out a hand to restrain her. 'Suppose it's Jack?'

'It could just as well be Guy,' she said, firmly putting aside his hand and lifting the receiver.

The next few seconds were some of the longest that James had experienced for some time.

'Yes, I'll hold on,' said Margaret, and then, 'Yes, I'll pay for the call.'

She shut her eyes and leaned back in her chair. James could guess nothing from the expression on her face.

At last she said, 'Yes, I'm home, darling. I'm all right, but the sooner you get here the better ... No, I'm not alone, I've got someone looking after me ... I'm all right, truly ... There's not much to eat in the house, so if you could bring some sandwiches and some milk it would help ... See you soon. God bless.'

She put down the phone and smiled at James, and he wondered if he was at last seeing the face of the real Margaret Leeming. Not beautiful, but very striking and intelligent. Very dark, very deep.

'Guy will be here soon,' she said. 'He's getting a taxi from the airport. He thought he'd better phone here before he got the London train to go to the clinic. Wasn't that lucky?'

'You mean he hasn't been in touch with the Windsor at all?'

'I don't think so. It looks as if nobody need know that you've been impersonating him.'

James had hardly time to express his relief when the telephone rang again. Margaret signed to him to leave it to her, picked up the receiver, but did not speak. James admired her self-control. There are not many people who can say nothing at all on an incoming call.

She listened for a moment or two and then replaced the receiver, all without having uttered a word.

'That was Jack,' she said. 'He'll probably try again. He thinks he's got a wrong number.'

'Silence and heavy breathing,' said James. 'It's usually the caller who indulges in them, not the recipient of the call.'

'I wasn't heavy breathing,' protested Margaret indignantly, 'and I think we'd better decide what to do with you in case Jack should decide to call in person. I've no idea where he was calling from. It could be anywhere between London and here.'

'But you came with me willingly,' said James. 'And in any case, Jack can't possibly know that it wasn't your husband who abducted you.'

'He could work it out. Guy couldn't possibly know that I was at Lark Heath.'

'Wait a minute—there's an answer to that. I know. I told Mrs. Kennedy that I was going to meet Guy at Gatwick. I could have met him and told him where you were. I as myself, I mean. Not I as Guy.'

James was beginning to feel very sleepy. Impersonating somebody was an exhausting business. No wonder spy stories were so often very confusing. It must be difficult for them to remember all the time who they were supposed to be.

Margaret got up and left the room. When she came back she said, 'If anybody comes who isn't Guy, then you must hide in the small guest-room. Come on. I'll show you now.'

The small guest-room, which was at the end of a long corridor and up a little winding staircase, looked so inviting that James wished he could remain there.

Margaret, reading his face, suggested that he should go to bed for what was left of the night.

'I want to be out of your way when Guy arrives,' said James, 'but if anybody else should turn up meanwhile—'

'I won't let them in. I promise.'

'But I don't like leaving you alone. You were going to tell me exactly what you remembered about being taken to the Windsor Clinic, when the phone call interrupted us. How about going back to it now?'

'I wonder if it's wise.' Margaret sat down on the edge of the bed. 'It might be better to try to convince them that I'm no danger to them.'

'But how?'

'I could work on Tony. He's less suspicious than Jack. If I can convince him that I really don't remember anything—'

'Then their plot will have succeeded and they will have got away with murder or whatever else it is they've been up to. I'm disappointed in you, Margaret Leeming.'

'You would prefer that I risk being treated as I have been this last week?'

'Of course not. Would I have gone to all

78

this trouble if I hadn't wanted to get you out of their clutches?'

James spoke unthinkingly, and then was appalled to find that they were actually shouting at each other, quarrelling quite heatedly.

How on earth had this come about? Could it be that he was more attracted to her than he realised? He certainly admired her, and he admired his own skill in carrying out his rescue plan, but he had been telling himself that he had been doing it all for Paula's sake.

'I'm sorry it's been such a burden to you,' Margaret was saying, 'but you'll soon be rid of me. Guy won't be long now.' She got up and walked to the door. 'Good night, James Goff. I'll leave it to Guy to do the thanking you tomorrow morning.'

'Oh Margaret, I'm sorry. I didn't mean—'

It wasn't often that James found himself at a loss for words. The attraction-repulsion mechanism seemed to be working more strongly than ever.

'Try and get some sleep,' she said. 'You'll find a toothbrush and other essentials in the bathroom. Good night.'

The door closed behind her. In a state of mounting agitation James explored the room and the neighbouring bathroom. All desire for sleep had fled. Never since the day when he first met Paula, nearly twenty years ago, had he been so intrigued by a woman as he was by Margaret Leeming. Not even during that strange sad time when he had planned to marry the girl who was his famous grandfather's step-daughter [*In* Last Judgement].

He stood at the window, from which he could see the light in the porch and the light at the front gate, and thought about Guy Leeming, that eminent elderly scholar who would be driving up any moment now in an airport cab. He must be nearly seventy. Twenty years older than Margaret at least. James had always admired his work, and from the little he knew him, liked him personally.

But as a husband for Margaret, Guy Leeming was surely lacking. A woman who had attracted that notorious surgeon, Jack Easebourne, and who was now so strongly attracting James himself ... If only Guy was not coming home tonight. Did Margaret feel that way too? He was almost sure that she did.

James made a great effort to take a grip on himself. This was not what had been envisaged when he promised Paula to help in any way he could. But it's Paula's fault in the first place, he thought, for getting involved in other people's affairs. Why does she always have to do it? She can't even recover from an operation in peace, as anybody else would.

Irritation with Paula momentarily

supplanted the pull of Margaret Leeming in his consciousness. If Paula would only consent to marriage, he told himself, it would all be different. They would then be completely committed to each other.

For a moment he believed this, and then honesty and the memory of past experience broke through, and he admitted that Paula had reason to be cautious. They were best as they were, with no formal tie, but over the years drawing ever more close in companionship, shared memories, and future hopes.

Standing by the window, expecting to see any moment the lights of Professor Leeming's taxi, James found himself positively relishing the mood of virtuous sentimentality into which he had slipped. Of course he would always be faithful to Paula. The very fact that she didn't expect it made it all the more necessary to convince her that he was a reformed character.

Margaret Leeming was an exception. He had not felt like this about any woman for a long time, and the extraordinary circumstances in which they had been brought together must surely account for it.

A knock at the door interrupted his incipient day-dreaming, but James still lingered by the window.

'Are you awake?'

Margaret's voice sounded tense and

anxious again.

James opened the door.

'I'm glad you haven't gone to bed,' she said. 'Would you mind coming down again until Guy comes? You were quite right. I don't feel happy there alone. The phone keeps ringing,' she explained as they negotiated the winding stair and the long corridor, 'and it's getting on my nerves.'

'Who is it calling? Always Jack?'

'Once again, and I did my no-talking act. And then it was a woman who sounded like the one at Lark Heath from whom you rescued me. Very nasty. She said, "I know perfectly well that you are there, Mrs. Leeming, and I warn you that these childish tricks will get you nowhere. There has been a serious offence committed this evening, and you and your accomplice will suffer for it."'

'Offence? Oh Lord. That means—'

'That they do after all know that you are you. Or rather, that you aren't Guy. I suppose the Lark Heath woman compared notes with the matron at the Windsor. You're taller than Guy, of course. And younger.'

They came back into the living-room.

'But that's not all,' went on Margaret. 'I've had Tony on the phone too.'

'Tony?'

'My brother. I don't know what part he's playing in all this, but he's been Jack's accountant for years and fiddled his tax for him.'

'Did you speak to Tony?'

'Of course. I feel more or less responsible for him since my sister-in-law died. And particularly for Emma. She's all right, thank God. Staying with some neighbours. And he's on his way here.'

'But it's gone one o'clock. It'll be nearly three by the time he arrives. Does he expect you to wait up all night for him?'

'I've no idea.' Margaret looked tired and ill again. Nothing remained of that little burst of radiance that had set off such a disturbing reaction in James.

'Shall I wait up for him?' he asked. 'I could try to deal with him for you.'

'I believe you could,' she replied. 'I'm taking that as a genuine offer, but I can't accept it. Tony's my responsibility.' She stood up. 'There's a car coming. That'll be Guy.'

She left the room, and after a moment's hesitation James followed her, telling himself that it was not safe to let her out of his sight until he was quite sure that no danger threatened, but in fact very glad of the chance to observe the greeting between herself and her husband.

He came out into the square, stone-flagged hall, and remained at some distance from the front door.

83

'I'll take your suitcase,' he heard Margaret say.

Damn the man, thought James; doesn't he realise that she's been ill?

Again she spoke. 'You must be worn out. Was the flight very much delayed?'

'A couple of hours.'

'Would you like anything to eat? Or will you go straight to bed?'

'I'll get to bed in a minute.'

Professor Leeming came within James's range of vision. He handed a bright red carrier bag to his wife, and said, 'I got some rolls and some milk. Had a long wait for them. That's why I'm late.'

Not one word, not one single word, thought James, about his wife and her ordeal. No concern for her at all.

Was this what the marriage was? A home and security for Margaret, and a companion-secretary-housekeeper and eventually nurse for Guy? Why had he assumed that it was a match of genuine affection? The answer came at once: because Margaret had played it that way. What an actress she was, and what a revelation it was when she let the act slip, as she was doing now.

She had made quite sure that James should see how matters really stood between her husband and herself. He was meant to be observing: that was why she had come up to

84

his room. At first she had not wanted him to see, had wanted to keep up the pretence. But she had changed her mind. And that must surely mean that she was as attracted to him as he was to her.

She was speaking now. Professor Leeming must at last have made some comment about his wife's road accident and her subsequent experiences which James, deep in his thoughts, had not heard.

'James drove me home from the nursing-home,' she said. 'You remember James Goff, darling?'

'Yes, of course.'

Guy came forward and they shook hands.

Away from the lecturer's rostrum, away from the aura of respect and admiration that surrounded him on his public appearances, he looked somehow diminished, greyer and older. It isn't fair to judge, James told himself; one always feels exhausted after returning from an American visit, especially if it includes a congress. He's jet-lagged, and he's worried about his wife.

Except that Guy didn't seem to be very much worried about his wife.

'It was very good of you to look after Margaret,' he was saying, 'but I cannot think why you should have been dragged into it at all. Nor why the clinic should discharge her at such short notice. The whole business is completely inexplicable.'

James felt a sudden surge of sympathy. Professor Leeming had every reason to feel bewildered. His information about Margaret's situation had come only through phone calls from her brother Tony, which meant that it would have been tailored entirely to suit Tony's convenience.

'It's my own fault, Guy,' said Margaret soothingly. 'They didn't want me to leave the clinic till tomorrow, but when I heard you were coming home tonight I was determined to be here. And James offered. He was visiting Paula Glenning, who was next door to me in the clinic. You remember Paula, darling, who wrote that excellent book about wives of famous authors.'

Guy Leeming, looking slightly less puzzled, said that of course he knew the book.

'But were you really fit to come home?' he added, looking at Margaret as if really seeing her for the first time since he had arrived. 'Tony said—'

'Don't take any notice of Tony,' Margaret interrupted him. 'You know he always makes the worst of things, and he's in rather a bad way himself. I'm going to try to persuade him to find a live-in housekeeper.'

'If you'd like Emma to come and live with us,' said Guy, moving into the living-room, 'you know I'd have no objection.'

Margaret followed him. 'I know, darling,

86

and I'd love to have her, but she doesn't want to leave her father and she loves her school.'

James felt that he ought to remove himself from this family discussion. 'If there's nothing I can do for you,' he said, 'I'd rather like to go to bed now.'

'Of course.' Margaret stood up again. 'I'll show you the guest-room.'

James forebore to remark that he knew where it was.

On the way upstairs Margaret said, 'You'll have guessed that I didn't want your protection. I just wanted you to meet Guy on his home ground.'

'Yes. I'd guessed that.'

'Don't misunderstand me. I'm perfectly contented in my marriage. I know my role and it suits me and I'm enormously grateful to Guy and wouldn't hurt him for the world. But you seemed to be under some extraordinary illusion that Guy was going to come back and sort out all my problems and take over completely. Confess it, James. Wasn't that what you were thinking?'

He confessed it.

'I can't imagine why you built up such a misapprehension,' said Margaret sharply. 'Guy knows nothing at all about my relationship with Jack Easebourne nor of the intrigues at the Windsor Clinic. There's no reason why he should be bothered with them. We live a very different sort of life here.'

James, tempted to speak equally sharply, managed to restrain himself. If he wasn't careful, they would be quarrelling again, and quarrels led to reconciliations, and reconciliations could be dangerous for two people so strongly attracted to each other.

'I understand,' he said. 'Truly I do. I'm sorry I'd built up such a false impression. Guy is to know nothing, and let's hope you can soon get back to your normal life. But if you do feel that you are still at risk, and if there is any way in which I can help you—'

He was not allowed to finish. Margaret was weeping on his shoulder and had to be comforted, and this continued for several minutes.

Then she drew away and said, 'I'm sorry. That wasn't the right moment to do that. I must get back to Guy. And I'm going to try to get a little sleep before Tony comes.'

'Tony—do you really think he's on his way?'

'I'm afraid so, but I don't want Guy to know.'

'How can you stop him knowing?'

'He'll go to bed soon, and he's a heavy sleeper.'

'Well, I'm not. At the moment I don't feel as if I'm ever going to sleep again, and certainly not until I've seen the end of this part of the drama. You do manage to get yourself into the most complicated situations, Margaret Leeming. You're even worse than Paula.'

'Paula,' she repeated, looking at him enquiringly.

James wished he had never mentioned her. He did not want to talk about Paula to Margaret. This might or might not be a bad sign, but it would definitely look odd if he refused to mention Paula at all, so he said, rather stiffly, 'I'll be glad when she's out of the clinic. I shall go straight there when I get back to London tomorrow morning.'

'To carry out another dramatic rescue?'

There was mockery in the voice and in the eyes.

'I wish she were fit to be moved now,' said James soberly. 'I'll feel much happier about her when she's in the convalescent home.'

'Paula will be all right provided she doesn't keep asking questions.'

And how does one stop Paula asking questions, was James's comment, but he did not make it aloud, and after thanking him again and hoping he would get some rest, Margaret left the room.

CHAPTER EIGHT

James awoke from an uneasy sleep. At first he thought he was on a train, because he still had his clothes on; and then the confusion cleared a little and he realised that he was lying on a bed, which one would not find on a train, and that there was no sound nor movement.

Memory returned. He found a light switch and looked round at the whitewashed walls, the leaf-patterned curtains, and the dormer window of Guy and Margaret Leeming's smaller guest-room.

The time was half past three. Margaret's brother Tony was due to arrive about now. Probably it had been the sound of his car that had awakened James. He got off the bed and looked out of the window. The lights in the porch and by the front gate were still shining, and on the drive between them, parked some distance from the house because James's Renault was blocking the way, was a second car, a long, square, hearse-like object, with quite a large dent in the side.

Volvo, thought James, who tended to judge people by the cars they drove; he's a bad driver and he wants to appear a much more confident and determined man than he really is.

He was pleased with his diagnosis, forgetting for the moment that it owed a lot to Paula's account of Tony Fielding's visit to her at the clinic. Very cautiously, and remembering to avoid a creaking floorboard, James made his way downstairs. Whether or not he would be able to overhear anything depended on where Margaret and her brother would be sitting.

If they were in the long low living-room it would be impossible, but James had a hope that they might have settled in the kitchen. He had had a quick sight of it when he first arrived with Margaret. It was a cosy old-fashioned kitchen, a good place for early hours of the morning confidences, and above all, it contained a serving hatch through which hot dishes could be handed to the dining-room next door.

James proposed to conceal himself in the darkness of the dining-room. He was in luck, and achieved his object without being heard or seen. The dining-room curtains were drawn back, and after waiting a few moments to allow his eyes to adjust to the dimness after the bright light in the hall, James found he could make out the shapes of pieces of furniture and could see where the serving-hatch was.

Its doors were closed, but there was a slit of light showing between them, and he could

91

hear the sound of voices coming from the kitchen. A dining-room chair was pushed against the wall. He sat down on it and put his ear to the doors of the hatch. A man's voice was speaking.

'I'll have to leave the country.'

'Where will you go? Spain is no good.'

It was Margaret Leeming speaking, but a different Margaret from any that James had yet heard: gentle and patient, but lacking the note of brightness that was so evident in her attitude towards her husband.

'No, Spain's no good anymore. It'll have to be South America.'

'Tony!' Her voice was alarmed. 'You've not got entangled with any of the drug barons?'

'Of course I haven't. The whole business is strictly medical, perfectly legitimate.'

'Then why—'

'Oh, you wouldn't understand. It's a question of the profits. How to account for them. Once they really get their teeth into my records—bloody vultures.'

There was a short silence, during which James thought he could hear the sound of crockery being moved. Then Margaret spoke again, in the same quietly unhappy manner.

'In other words, you've been laundering profits from the sale of drugs. What Mother and Dad would have thought, if they'd known.'

'I didn't choose to. I've told you. Jack dragged me in. I'd not the slightest idea where the money was coming from until it was too late to get out.'

James, listening intently, felt almost relieved as he took in what Margaret and her brother were saying. A little corner of the drugs trade, operated by a dishonest accountant, a greedy and totally unscrupulous medical man, and a posh private nursing-home. This made sense, which the vague theory that Margaret had witnessed a murder did not, and in the light of this revelation the persecution of Margaret made sense too. They were afraid she was going to expose them.

Tony was continuing to protest that he didn't know about it until it was too late.

'You might have tried,' said Margaret. The tenderness was still there in her voice, but there was another note as well. Could it be anger, or was she just teasing her brother?

'Jack would have murdered me,' Tony said.

'So you let him try to murder me instead?'

'You weren't to come to any real harm.'

There was no doubt what Tony was feeling. He had none of his sister's histrionic powers, and the complaining, self-pitying tones in which he spoke so disgusted James that he could barely sit still in his hiding-place.

'Your memory had been affected by the concussion in any case, and so long as it remained unreliable—'

'Are you telling me that to lose one's wits does not count as "any real harm"?'

Margaret's voice rose as she spoke. James could not distinguish any of the words in Tony's mumbled reply. There followed a short silence, in which James pictured the two of them sitting at the kitchen table, staring at each other.

Tony was the first to speak again. 'You never told me how you found out about it.'

'You ought not to have asked me to stay with you and Emma, and then go and leave your desk unlocked.'

'You mean you were snooping round my room?'

'As a matter of fact I was looking for a photo of Linda for Emma. She thought it might be in one of the drawers of your desk.'

'You always were an interfering little bitch.'

Tony had raised his voice too. James tried not to listen to the subsequent exchanges. It sounded like a repeat of many quarrels between brother and sister, probably going right back to the very earliest years.

An only child himself, and a very over-indulged one, James had no personal experience of this sort of thing and it always rather embarrassed him. The fact that he was

94

eavesdropping, however, did not cause him any qualms of conscience at all. At one point he even wondered if Margaret had planned this too, knowing that James would go to any lengths to find out why Tony had come, but he abandoned this theory on the grounds that Margaret could not have known that he would wake up at the right moment and find a suitable place to conceal himself.

Was he going to let her know what he had overheard? It was too early to decide. He must listen again: they were finished with the abuse and had returned to the essentials.

Margaret was speaking; she was asking Tony how much Linda—presumably Tony's wife and Emma's mother—had known about it.

'Linda was never involved,' Tony insisted. 'As if I'd let her run the risk.'

'She'd have had to be involved if you'd been arrested and come to trial,' retorted Margaret. 'How do you know that she didn't know about it? Of course she did. It was the strain and worry of it that caused her nervous breakdown.'

Nervous breakdown, repeated James silently to himself; that's the first I've heard of it. I wonder if Paula knows. He listened carefully again to the brother and sister talking about Tony's wife, and gathered that her untimely death had not been caused by a serious illness or fatal road accident, but by an overdose of tranquillisers taken while she was suffering one of her depressive attacks.

Accidentally taken, of course. No blame attached to anybody. Paula certainly didn't know about this, James said to himself, and his thoughts went to Emma with great pity and concern; he longed to do something to help the child, and determined to talk to Paula about it.

The two people talking in the kitchen next door were speaking more and more quietly. Perhaps they had got up from the table and moved further away from the serving-hatch. James waited and listened, but could hear no further sound. Had they gone somewhere else to continue their talk? Or had Margaret guessed that they were being overheard? And above all, what was she going to do?

Suddenly James was overpowered by a sense of urgency and a great longing to take the decisions himself.

They must hold on to Tony Fielding now at all costs and call the police immediately. Brother or no brother, there were no two ways about it. Here was a chance to break up a tiny corner of one of the most repulsive activities ever thought up by human greed, and no family or personal considerations ought to enter into it at all. Although of course he could understand why Margaret had kept quiet and tried to handle it herself; perhaps if he had been in a similar position, and it was somebody very close to him, he might have been tempted to do the same.

James reached the door of the dining-room. He pulled it open, not caring now whether he was discovered.

There was nobody in the hall. He looked towards the living-room. The door was open and the room in darkness.

Surely they would not have gone upstairs? He walked up a few steps, then turned round again and came down the steps to find himself face to face with Margaret.

'What's happening? Are you all right?' he asked. He felt guilty and self-conscious and was quite sure that he looked it.

'Of course I'm all right.'

'I was woken up by some noise or other and thought I'd better come down and investigate,' continued James lamely. 'Has he come?'

'Who?'

'Tony. Your brother. You were expecting him to arrive about now.'

'Was I?'

Ah, thought James, so it's to be outright denial and the playing of a lone game by Margaret. Should he go along with it, conceal his own knowledge, not even tell Paula? After all, Paula's main concern was that somebody should rescue Margaret, and that he had triumphantly achieved. Margaret was now a free agent; she must make her own choices and take responsibility for herself.

'If you don't need my help, then I'll go back to bed,' he said abruptly.

'Yes. You do that.'

He turned away without another word and managed to get halfway up the first flight of stairs before giving way to the impulse to look back. She was leaning against the stair-rail, clinging to it as if she needed its support, and looking up at him. James glanced down at her face and thought he had seldom seen an expression of such desolation. Why could she not ask for help? Was it pride? Or a reluctance to involve him in her own danger? Or a fear, like his own, of becoming emotionally involved?

But whatever her motive, it made no difference now. To turn round at that moment had been fatal, and yet he had not been able to help doing so.

He ran downstairs and put an arm round her shoulders. 'Come and tell me about it. Where shall we go? In here?'

He indicated the door of the living-room.

'Yes.' She pulled herself away and walked slowly and stiffly to a chair. 'Don't be afraid,' she went on as he stood uncertainly in front of her, 'that I'm going to collapse on you. Just sit and listen. This time we are going down to rock-bottom truth. Although I suspect that you already know quite a lot of it.'

She looked at him enquiringly. James lowered his head.

'I thought so,' said Margaret. 'Where were you? Ah yes. In the dining-room, of course. You must have noticed the serving-hatch.'

She leaned back and began to laugh. 'After all my efforts to stop you from finding out,' she managed to say before the hysterical laughter engulfed her completely. It seemed to James after a while that his attempts to comfort and quieten her would have more success upstairs in the small guest-room than down in the living-room, and this assumption proved to be quite correct.

CHAPTER NINE

Paula could hear herself crying out as she struggled to sit up.

'No, no! I won't take the tablets!'

Somebody was gripping her shoulders, shaking her, almost smothering her. She tried to scream, and then remembered that she must keep her mouth shut. That was her only hope.

The fear and the horror increased beyond endurance. She struggled out of the nightmare at last and woke to find herself sweating and shuddering, clutching at the bedclothes, which were in great disorder. A pillow was slipping to the floor. Paula twisted round hastily to try to catch it, and immediately felt so sick and giddy that she could do nothing but lean back again while waves of nausea attacked her.

There was mounting panic too. She had never felt so ill as this, not even when first coming round from the anaesthetic. It was as bad as the nightmare, but she knew that she was fully awake. Perhaps this was normal after the operation; or perhaps something had gone wrong.

The need for reassurance became overwhelming. She stretched out her left hand and felt for the bell-push. There would be two night nurses on duty. She waited in ever-increasing impatience and apprehension for the arrival of a trained professional. Her adult mind was telling her that there could not be anything seriously wrong, but the infantile panic would not be stilled.

The door opened and somebody switched on the bedside lamp.

'You rang, Mrs. Glenning. What can I do for you?'

It was the cold clear voice of Mrs. Kennedy, and it brought very little comfort to Paula apart from making her wonder why the matron should be answering the bell when the agency nurse had said that she had been called away, and this little problem took Paula's mind off her own condition for a minute or two.

'I was having a bad nightmare,' she said, 'and I woke feeling very ill, but it's easing off now.'

The nausea did indeed seem to be receding, and reason and caution were reasserting themselves. Had it been Louise, or one of the agency night nurses, Paula would have told them her fears. But not the matron, who was not to be trusted at all.

Mrs. Kennedy laid a cool hand on Paula's forehead and then took hold of her wrist.

'You are slightly feverish,' she said, 'but it's not unusual at this stage and is nothing to worry about. I'll bring you something to help you go back to sleep.'

'Thank you,' said Paula meekly. 'And could I please have some tea?'

'Of course. I'll fetch it for you.'

The matron rearranged Paula's bedclothes quickly and efficiently, helped her to sit up against the pillows, and left the room. By the time she returned, five minutes later, Paula had recovered her self-control and had come to a decision.

'Feeling better now?' said Mrs. Kennedy brightly as she placed a small tray on the bedside table.

'Much better, thanks,' replied Paula, wondering whether her own voice sounded as false as the matron's.

'Sugar?'

'No thanks.'

Paula watched Mrs. Kennedy pour milk and tea into a rather pretty blue and green cup. On a spare saucer alongside lay a couple of small white tablets.

'Just take one now,' said the matron, holding out the saucer to Paula, 'and you can have the second one later on if you wake again.'

Paula picked up one of the tablets and put it into her mouth. It lodged itself, as she had planned, in a broken tooth which she intended to take to the dentist as soon as she was well enough. She was aware that the matron was looking at her very closely, and she felt an almost uncontrollable desire to laugh, remembering the occasion when James had tried to administer a pill to his black cat. With a great effort she controlled herself, and holding the tablet in place with her tongue, took a drink from the teacup and succeeded in swallowing the tea without shifting the tablet.

But her hand was shaking as she replaced the cup, and it tipped and spilt tea all over the tray. Mrs Kennedy, with an exclamation of annoyance, turned away from Paula to attend to the spillage, and taking advantage of this unexpected bonus, Paula removed the tablet from her mouth and put her hand under the bedclothes.

102

'I'm awfully sorry,' she murmured, sliding down further into the bed. 'I'm almost asleep already. I don't think I shall need...'

She left the sentence unfinished, turned over, and shut her eyes. Through half-closed eyes Paula saw the matron pick up the tray and notice that the second tablet was rapidly dissolving in the split tea. She hesitated for a few seconds and then left the room, muttering under her breath that 'it didn't matter—one would be enough.'

Paula waited until she heard the door close, and then she turned over, switched on the light again, and sat up.

One would be enough. Enough for what?

The sickness and giddiness had almost entirely left her, and she felt alert and very suspicious. Enough for what? To send her to sleep again? Or was there a less innocent intention?

Now don't panic, she told herself severely. As far as the matron knows, you've swallowed another sleeping pill and will remain asleep for several hours. Louise will be coming on duty at eight and you can ask her about it. And James will be getting in touch.

Paula's thoughts drifted from her own situation into speculation about James. It was less than twelve hours since he had left her, but it seemed like days ago. Had he succeeded in finding out where Margaret

103

had been taken? Had he managed to get in touch with Guy Leeming? And above all, where was he now?

At this point she must have fallen asleep, because when she once more became conscious of her surroundings, the green and yellow curtains looked brilliantly transparent in the bright morning sunshine and the matron was standing by the bed with a cup of tea.

Paula rubbed a hand over her eyes and very slowly raised herself into a half-sitting position. So the tablet I didn't take wasn't actually meant to kill me, she thought; obviously I'm still supposed to be alive if she's brought me tea.

It seemed wise, however, to appear more drowsy than she really felt, and she rubbed her eyes again and murmured, 'Tea—how lovely.'

'You've had a good sleep?'

It was more a statement than a question.

'Yes, thanks,' said Paula.

'That's fine,' said Mrs. Kennedy, smiling with her mouth but not with her eyes. 'Now I can tell you some good news. The convalescent home can take you in today. There's no need to wait until tomorrow as originally planned. And there's no need to worry about transport either. Mr Easebourne will be driving down himself later this morning to see a patient there, and he will be quite happy to convey you. He's a careful driver, and if you should feel any ill effects from the journey, you couldn't be in safer hands.'

'But I'd already arranged with my friend James Goff,' began Paula and then stopped abruptly. Mrs. Kennedy's last words had so surprised and shocked her that she could feel her hand begin to shake as she sipped at her tea. Hurriedly she replaced the cup on the saucer that lay on the bedside table, and hoped that her agitation was not too noticeable.

'He'll be coming here later this morning,' she went on, quite calmly, finding it easier to control her voice than her movements, 'and I wouldn't want him to come and find me gone.'

'There's no need to worry about that,' said Mrs. Kennedy quickly. 'Mr. Goff has been on the phone already this morning and is quite in agreement with the changed arrangements.'

She's lying, said Paula to herself, and she's not a very good liar.

'I see,' she said aloud in a surprisingly steady voice. 'Then what time do you want me to be ready, and please could one of the nurses come and help me to pack?'

'Of course.' Matron smiled again, and Paula thought she looked relieved that there was apparently to be no further protest.

'There is no great hurry. After breakfast someone will come and help you.'

Paula smiled back and took another sip of tea. Her hand was quite steady now and her mind was working quickly. As soon as Mrs. Kennedy had left the room she lifted the phone and dialled James's number. There was no reply, but she succeeded in holding back her panic. She had been quite prepared for this. James was no doubt still running about on the Margaret Leeming business. Or else he had got back very late the night before and was still fast asleep. At any rate she was more convinced than ever that Mrs. Kennedy had not been in touch with him.

She was just about to fall back on her second line of defence when a nurse came in with her breakfast tray. Paula replaced the telephone and smiled up at her. She was a tall red-haired girl called Carol who occasionally did a morning duty.

'Thanks,' Paula said, and added very casually, 'Is Louise on duty today?'

'Not till this afternoon,' replied Carol, puffing up the pillows. 'She was to be on this morning but Matron asked her to switch to the afternoon because one of the other nurses particularly wanted to be free then.'

'I see,' said Paula, refraining from adding that she saw all too clearly how Matron had arranged for Louise to be absent until Paula was safely out of the way. Not that I would

106

have asked her to help me, thought Paula; I wouldn't want her to risk losing her job. 'Are you going to help me pack, Carol?' she asked aloud.

'When you're ready,' replied the girl. 'There's no need to hurry.'

'Then give me half an hour, would you,' said Paula, 'to finish my breakfast and get washed and dressed. Thanks.'

As soon as the nurse had gone, Paula picked up the telephone again and began to dial her sister's number. But after the first three digits she hesitated and then replaced the receiver. Stella would come to the rescue, would even offer to look after her, but Paula was very reluctant to burden her so much. With a full-time teaching job, two school-age children, and a husband who wasn't much help with the household chores, Stella had enough to do without taking on a barely convalescent sister as well, particularly when that sister had once again been meddling in other people's affairs, and this at a time when she was far too weak to cope with such matters.

'I can't tell Stella,' muttered Paula, picking up the telephone again. 'There must be some other way.' Emma's friends? Just as a temporary measure, a few hours' security while she found another nursing-home that would take her in.

No. No good. No other nursing-home

would give her a bed without medical recommendation, and they certainly wouldn't believe her story of being in danger at the prestigious Windsor Clinic.

Her own doctor who had arranged for the operation in the first place? But he was away on holiday, and Paula hardly knew the other partners in the general practice.

What about Miss Twigg, the surgeon who was supposed to have done the op? She was away on sick leave, but it wasn't a serious illness. Surely Paula could telephone her home number and make a personal appeal? Miss Twigg knew the Windsor Clinic well. She might even have her own suspicions. She and Paula had become quite friendly during the consultations, and Miss Twigg had given Paula her home phone number.

This was written in Paula's diary, which was in her handbag. She reached out to take it from the shelf in the bedside table, and at that moment the phone rang.

'Hi, Paula? Are you all right? I've been trying to get you for ages.'

The relief of hearing James's voice was overwhelming.

'Where are you?' she asked.

'I'm at home. I got back about an hour ago. Everything's going fine. Margaret's safe, and Guy—'

Paula interrupted. 'Sorry, darling, I'm dying to hear all, but there's no time to lose.

108

Could you come round here right away?'

'More problems?'

'Yes. Very urgent.'

'I'll be there. Ten minutes.'

James didn't stop to ask questions. Paula could feel the tears stinging her eyes. She had not realised until the danger was almost over how heavily she had been drawing on her tiny reserves of strength. Resisting the over-powering urge to lean back and go to sleep again, she struggled into her clothes, crept into the bathroom, and wiped her face with a damp cloth before returning to collapse into the armchair by the side of the bed. To make any further effort was at that moment beyond her. If Carol didn't come back in time, then James would have to pack her things.

She shut her eyes and tried to relax. Her racing heart seemed to be slowing down a little when she suddenly remembered that she had intended to retrieve whatever was left of the tablet that she had not swallowed last night. It would be interesting to find out whether it contained the drug that had been used on Margaret Leeming to encourage loss of memory and mental confusion, or whether it was indeed a harmless sleeping pill.

She raised herself up a little in the chair so that she could stretch out an arm and feel under the pillow and along the bottom sheet, but hastily withdrew her hand when she heard footsteps in the corridor. Could it be James already? He had said ten minutes, and his flat was not far away.

Paula shut her eyes. The footsteps slowed down and there came a faint creaking sound as the door was opened. Paula's hearing, always acute, was heightened by the tension of suspense. Her heart began to race again as she waited for the sound of a voice. If it's Matron to say that Mr. Easebourne has come for me early, she was saying to herself, whatever excuse can I make?

For the moment she could think of nothing better than to pretend to be asleep, but she was still listening intently.

'Mrs. Glenning,' she heard the matron say, 'I've come to tell you—'

The false brightness of the voice was more marked than ever. Paula kept her eyes closed. Her heart was racing again, and she was so intent on finding an excuse for delay that she did not notice the second set of footsteps; it took a few seconds to register that there was another person in the room, interrupting Mrs. Kennedy in a rather breathless voice.

'I'm very sorry to disturb you, Matron, but there's a very urgent phone call for you.'

'All right, I'll come. Stay here, Carol, and help Mrs. Glenning to get ready.'

'Yes, Matron,' said the girl meekly.

There was a pause and the sound of movement. Then Paula judged it was safe to open her eyes. The young nurse was standing in the doorway, looking at her in some puzzlement.

'Do you mind,' she said as Paula glanced up at her, 'waiting for a minute or two? I've got a patient urgently needing a bedpan and—'

'No hurry at all,' replied Paula quickly. 'In any case, I can manage by myself.'

She dragged herself up from the chair, but the girl had gone without waiting to hear her out.

Paula thought quickly. There wasn't much time to spare. No doubt the plan had been to lull her into false security for a couple of hours and then hustle her away.

James would be here any minute now. It was almost fifteen minutes since he had phoned. If she wasn't so weak she'd go herself to the front door of the clinic and wait for him there. But someone would be bound to see her and in any case she'd probably collapse in the street.

What else could she do? Pretend to be too ill to be moved? No, that wouldn't work.

Another way out of the clinic? Emma's way? Through the gap in the fence and the garden of the house next door. Had she the strength for that?

Paula opened the French window and sat

down on the end of the bed. She'd recognise James's footsteps, and if she heard anybody else approaching she would go out into the garden and try Emma's way. There were taxis near the clinic. At the very worst she would get into one and go to Stella.

Saturday morning. Somebody would be at home. And if not, then she would try Emma's friends. In fact she would try them first: they would be nearer. And somehow or other she would get a message to James to tell him where she was.

Don't panic, she told herself firmly: you've got your plan for emergency action all ready; you are not, repeat, not going to be taken away by Jack Easebourne to whatever he has planned for you.

But it was very difficult to keep calm. Paula got up from the bed, opened the door, and looked down the corridor. Nobody was in sight, and for a moment she was tempted to make a dash for the entrance. She restrained herself, propped open the door, and returned to her place to listen intently for the sound of anyone approaching. James's footsteps she would certainly recognise, and she believed she could distinguish between the young nurse's quick walk and the matron's weightier step.

In fact she was taken by surprise. Her attention must have wandered or perhaps she had even fallen momentarily asleep.

Carol and James came into the room together.

'I'll help Mrs. Glenning,' said James immediately to Carol. 'There's no need for you to stay.'

'But Matron said—'

'That's all right. I've had a word with her, and I'm driving Mrs. Glenning to the convalescent home myself.'

'Well I am rather rushed at the moment—'

Carol didn't take much persuading to leave.

James opened the closet door and took out Paula's suitcase.

'There's no time!' cried Paula, pulling at his arm. 'And we'll have to get out Emma's way—quick! Before they come.'

James began to protest that he could handle Mrs. Kennedy and also Mr. Easebourne if need be, but seeing Paula's extreme distress, gave way and joined her at the window.

'Which way?' he asked, closing it behind him.

'Right. Round the end of the building.' Paula spoke in little gasps as they moved along. 'Emma said keep close to the bushes.'

'And here's the gap in the hedge.'

It was quite a wide gap, but the broken palings that straddled the ground made walking difficult, and James decided that it was wise to carry Paula through.

'I'm all right now,' she murmured as they came out among the shrubs in the neighbouring garden. 'You'd better go and check that there's no one about.'

James explored cautiously.

'There's no one about, and there's a "For Sale" notice. It looks as if the place is unoccupied, but I think you'd better wait here while I bring the car round. You'll be much too exposed sitting on the wall by the front gate.'

'Don't be long,' murmured Paula, propping herself up against the lower branches of a large rhododendron bush.

During his absence she shut her eyes and relaxed as best she could, but the relief of having escaped from the clinic was almost outweighed by the worry that she might be delaying her own recovery.

'I'm only supposed to walk up and down the corridor and a little way round the garden,' she said to herself, 'and I'm going to need looking after for another week. What on earth are we going to do?'

The sound of a car's engine interrupted her anxious thoughts. Paula roused herself and pushed forward between the shrubs.

James's Renault had pulled up in the drive, and he was getting out and coming towards her.

'You must be crazy, to take such a risk,' she murmured, conscious that she was in danger of laughing uncontrollably, and struggling to steady herself.

'We're both crazy,' he said as he backed the car down the drive.

'I ought to explain,' Paula began after successfully holding back the threatened hysteria.

'Not now. Tell me later. Try to rest,' said James.

'I will,' she replied, 'if you'll tell me where we are going. I thought perhaps I could go home and get in an agency nurse to—'

'You'll have a nurse,' James interrupted as they came out into the road. 'We're going down to Sussex, to Guy and Margaret Leeming. Guy got back last night and we got Margaret out of their clutches and she's fine now and will look after you till you're able to fend for yourself.'

'But I can't intrude,' protested Paula.

'Nonsense. They'll be delighted to help you. Out of gratitude if nothing else. If you hadn't been so inquisitive about the patient next door then I'd never have become involved and God knows what would have happened to Margaret Leeming. No, my love, I'm not going to tell you the story of last night's rescue. You're much too tired to listen. We'll get you back to bed, and when you're feeling stronger we'll have a council of war and pool our discoveries and see if we can find out what the hell is going on at the

115

Windsor Clinic.'

'I'm beginning to think—' Paula was indeed exhausted, but her mind was still active.

'Please, darling, not now. I've had hardly any sleep myself and I need to concentrate on the traffic.'

Paula subsided and actually did doze a little when they got out of London. But when James pulled in by a public telephone and got out to make a call, she woke up and began to think, not about the mystery centred on the Windsor Clinic, but about James himself.

The relief of getting away and having James take care of her had been so great that it blotted out all other thoughts. But now that the immediate danger was over and she felt more steady and a little less exhausted, there was leisure to think about James.

She knew him very well indeed, his variations of mood, the times when he could be cajoled and persuaded and the times when there would be no moving him. And she also knew how to recognise the times when he was being completely open and sincere, and the times when he was hiding something. There was probably nobody else who could recognise the signs, but Paula always could, and she had never been wrong yet.

He was hiding something now. It might be

116

something important or it might be something quite trivial. Almost certainly he was doing it for her sake, because he didn't think she was strong enough to face up to whatever it was. Paula did not feel fit at the moment to absorb any more shocks, but that did not mean that her reasoning powers were in abeyance. She would go along with whatever James suggested, or whatever the others suggested when they arrived at the Leemings' house, and she would show nothing but gratitude and a desire to unravel the Windsor Clinic affair; but underneath it all, at the very heart of herself, she would be observing and noting.

James returned from making his phone call.

'That's all right,' he said, just a trifle too heartily. 'They're getting a room ready for you and as soon as you feel fit for it, you shall hear everything.'

'Thanks, darling,' said Paula sleepily. 'I think I'll doze a bit now.'

But every now and then she opened her eyes to take a sideways glance at James's face, and she noticed that he did not refer to the map nor show any hesitation about finding the way to the Leemings' house.

CHAPTER TEN

'Are we there already?'

Paula had been dreaming, something to do with the rhythm of the car, and woke with a start when they slowed down.

'Do I look very awful, James? I haven't even brushed my hair.'

'This isn't a social visit,' he replied laughing. 'You're here as a refugee. In any case, you look surprisingly perky, considering the events of the last few hours.'

'I'm longing to have a bath.'

'You shall have it, and anything else you want.'

'But what about the clinic? They'll be looking for me—suppose they tell the police?'

'There's no need to worry about that yet. Your job now is to rest and get well.'

'Please, James.' Paula's voice was firm. She was fully awake now and had taken a good look at the long low flint-faced house a few yards further along the road. 'Don't be so condescending. Of course I've got to give myself a chance to recover, but it doesn't mean that I'm incapable of rational thinking or that I don't want to know what's going on. Understand?'

'Completely.' James leant across to kiss

her. 'You are to be present at all councils of war and have your full say before any decision is taken.'

'Thanks.'

James started the car again and turned into the drive. He's feeling embarrassed and he's rather dreading our arrival, said Paula to herself. Why? The best answer she could give herself was that the Leemings were reluctant to have her stay with them and James had over-persuaded them.

This made sense. It was asking a lot of any couple to take in somebody in Paula's condition; and in this case the husband had only just returned from a long and tiring American visit, and the wife had been in a road accident and been badly treated at the clinic, and if it hadn't been for Paula herself...

The memory of her meeting with Margaret in the room next door came vividly to Paula's mind and brought reassurance. Margaret would surely want to help her. The awkwardness must come from her husband, whom James knew only in his public capacity and Paula didn't know at all.

It was Professor Guy Leeming who opened the door to them. Paula had the impression of somebody older than she had expected, who didn't appear at all formidable, but actually rather bewildered. James was introducing her.

119

'Dr. Paula Glenning, whose book about my famous grandfather came out a couple of years ago.'

Professor Leeming's face took on a look of comprehension, almost of relief. He shook hands with Paula. 'Your study of G. E. Goff—of course I read it. A most original method of approach. Not that I approve in general of laying too much stress on the domestic life of genius, but in your case—'

'Guy darling.' Margaret Leeming came running across the hall. 'I'm afraid you'll have to postpone the academic discussion. Paula has to rest.'

'But I'd love to talk to Professor Leeming—it's such a pleasure to meet him.'

Paula managed to speak clearly, although everything seemed to be swaying and fading around her. If James had not been holding her she would have fallen.

Margaret rushed forward to take his place. Paula felt the warmth of her arms and heard, as if from a great distance, the reassuring voice as they moved slowly upstairs.

'You'll be all right presently. It's over-exertion, that's all. A slight recurrence of post-operative shock. Don't try to talk now. I'll bring you some tea. I promise you it won't last long.'

'I feel such a nuisance,' muttered Paula.

'You're not a nuisance.' Margaret sat down on the edge of the bed beside her and

120

put her arms around her. 'I'm just so glad you're safe. And I'm grateful for a chance to thank you. So is Guy. He's longing to talk literary criticism with you, but don't let him tire you out.'

Margaret stood up. 'I'll fetch that tea. Here's your bathroom.' She opened a door. 'And nightgown if you want to go straight to bed. When you feel a bit rested you must make a list of the things you want from your flat, and one of us will go up to London to fetch them.'

Suddenly she smiled, and Paula, feeling less giddy now, happened to look up at the same moment. She was struck by the transformation in Margaret's face. She was wearing light grey trousers and a white shirt, but Paula could imagine her dressed in vivid colours—scarlet or emerald perhaps. For anybody who appreciated vitality and strength she would outshine any more conventional beauty. Paula felt that she fully understood now for the first time why a philanderer like Jack Easebourne had been attracted to her.

'It all seems so unreal,' Paula said. 'The clinic, I mean. Margaret, can we possibly be imagining that they were trying to dope us into a state where anything we said would not be believed? Are we imagining it?'

'No, we certainly aren't imagining it, and if we'd got any sense we'd leave the whole business alone now, but of course we aren't going to.'

'It's so absurd, having someone trying to dope you out of your mind when you don't even know what it is that they think you know.'

Paula, lying back comfortably on the bed now, was already beginning to feel a lot better, and was almost disappointed when Margaret changed the subject, suggesting that she should call her own doctor to check that all was well with Paula.

'I don't think your exertions have done any damage, but you're not really fit to be discharged just yet and I'd like Dr. Wimborne to see you.'

Paula was obliged to agree, but after Margaret had gone she got up from the bed and began to inspect her surroundings, going first to the bathroom, which was adequate but not ostentatious, and then to the casement window with its pleasantly open view across fields and hedges. The wheat looked ripe for harvesting and she could hear the song of a lark ascending. To her right was a little group of cottages, half hidden by trees, and further in the distance was the spire of a church.

For the first time since the operation Paula had a sense of peace and security, and with it came a feeling that some big change was about to occur in her life, perhaps for the better, perhaps for the worse, but in either case it felt as if there was no avoiding it.

This feeling of unresisting acceptance didn't last for long. Natural curiosity reasserted itself, and by the time Margaret returned with a tea-tray Paula had looked at the furniture and the pictures, and was sitting in a low wickerwork chair by the side of a bookcase, making her selection from a shelf full of crime and mystery stories.

'James is going to collect your things,' said Margaret. 'He'll be up in a minute to take instructions.'

'I'm afraid I've not thought about it,' said Paula, gratefully accepting the tea. 'But it doesn't matter—he'll know what to bring and he's got a key to the flat. There's no need for him to come up—could you give him my love and thanks and tell him I've gone to sleep?'

'All right. Bang on the floor if you need anything. Either Guy or I will hear. And have a good rest.'

Margaret said no more, but after she had gone away Paula had the feeling that in this short conversation they had in fact conveyed a great deal to each other. She didn't want to analyse it too closely. She only knew that at this moment she didn't want to talk to James. Later on, when she felt more adjusted to her present circumstances, she would probably feel differently.

Downstairs in the long low sitting-room, James was walking up and down impatiently. The telephone rang for the fourth time in the last ten minutes, and automatically he moved towards the extension that stood on the coffee table. After two rings it was silent, and a moment later Guy came into the room, looking both annoyed and alarmed.

'Some moronic joker,' he complained, 'puts the phone back the moment I answer it. Where's Margaret?'

'Upstairs with Paula,' replied James. 'She'll be down in a minute. Why don't you cut off the extension in your study, and I'll answer if it rings again.'

'Thanks,' said Guy, somewhat mollified. 'I'm expecting a couple of calls from London, but this silly business—' He broke off and paused a moment before continuing. 'What's your private opinion, James? Do you really believe that Margaret was drugged and kept in a nursing-home because she knew too much?' These last words were spoken with a mock melodramatic emphasis.

'I've not the least doubt of it,' replied James robustly. 'And if we hadn't rescued Paula this morning she'd have been due for the same treatment.'

'It all sounds quite absurd.'

'It does, doesn't it? But if you'd seen that place last night—'

Unexpectedly Professor Leeming began to

laugh. 'I'd like to have seen your impersonation of me.'

James looked embarrassed. 'It was the only thing to do, but I'm a bit ashamed of it. I'd rather Paula didn't know, so if you don't mind keeping up the pretence with her that you fetched Margaret yourself—'

'I don't mind, if that's how you want it.' Guy moved towards the door, but when he had reached it he paused and turned back. 'Margaret swears it's nothing to do with that wretched brother of hers, but I feel sure he's at the bottom of this. A wrong 'un if ever there was one.'

'I don't know anything about him,' said James cautiously, 'except that Paula told me she didn't take to him, and she's usually a good judge of people.'

'So is Margaret.' Guy seemed about to say something more, but the telephone rang again and he hurriedly left the room.

'Hullo,' said James into the mouthpiece, 'Who do you want to speak to?'

There was no reply but neither did the line go dead.

'If it's Mrs. Leeming you want, and if you'll hang on for a moment, I can hear her coming now.' He put the phone down carefully on the table and went into the hall to tell Margaret about the calls.

'Stay with me,' she murmured to James as she picked up the phone. After listening for a

125

moment she said, very firmly, 'Yes, I'm alone. You can say whatever it is you need to say.'

James, standing near to her, could hear the voice at the other end of the line, but he could neither identify it nor make out what it was saying.

'I promise you nobody else is listening,' repeated Margaret. 'What is it you want to tell me?'

She listened again. James, giving up the attempt to hear anything, moved back a little and saw the expression on Margaret's face change from firm resolution to doubt and anxiety.

'Is your mother there?' she asked eventually, waited for the answer, and then put her hand over the mouthpiece and whispered to James, 'Emma's disappeared— it's her friend Jasmine.'

She removed her hand and listened again. After a while she said, 'Thank you very much indeed for phoning me, Jasmine. Will you let me know if you have any further news? I'm going to be in all day, so if my husband answers the phone, please ask him to call me. And try not to worry too much. It isn't your fault or your mother's ... Of course it isn't. Most likely Emma is with her father and I shall be hearing from them later today. I'll let you know if I do. Right away. I promise faithfully.'

Margaret listened again and then repeated her promise.

'Hurry up and tell me,' said James impatiently when she replaced the phone.

Margaret sat down and looked at him unhappily, but she said nothing.

'I suppose your wretched brother, as Guy calls him, has flown off to his bolt-hole taking Emma with him,' said James irritably.

'I don't know, I rather doubt it,' muttered Margaret.

'Why?' demanded James.

'Because Tony wouldn't do anything so decisive.'

'Then where is he? And, more important, where is Emma?'

Margaret looked even more wretched. 'I don't know.'

James fought back the impulse to comfort her. The last thing they needed was for him and Margaret to be discovered in a close embrace. That Paula would come downstairs just yet was most unlikely, but Guy seemed to be very restless and was certainly not concentrating on the pile of correspondence that had accumulated while he was away.

James, in the midst of his own preoccupation, had a momentary stab of sympathy for Guy, returning from an exhausting trip to find his home life very disrupted.

'Is there anything I can usefully do,' he

asked, 'while I'm in London fetching Paula's things? I'll certainly go and see Emma's friends,' he went on, since Margaret remained silent, 'and I don't mind calling in at the clinic. I shall tell them I've taken Paula to stay with friends who will look after her, and I'll see if I can find out what—'

'That's a good idea.'

The voice was Guy's, and it came from behind James, who was standing with his back to the half open door and had not heard anybody come in. Although relieved that he had not been saying anything that could arouse any suspicions in Guy, he felt a growing sense of having acted unwisely in bringing Paula here at all.

His own idea had been to take Paula back to his flat and get an agency nurse in to look after her while they found out whether Miss Twigg was fit to return to work. Margaret had persuaded him against this. He could not stand up to her arguments; he was too bewitched by her. One moment she seemed warmly responsive, the next moment she was darkly mysterious, withdrawn from him and unapproachable. As Emma, that intelligent and perceptive child, had said, her aunt was a very good actress, and James could only guess at her real motive for wanting Paula in her home.

Was it to prove to Guy that she was concerned only for Paula and had no particular interest in Paula's man? Or was it for the opposite reason—that she was afraid of losing James's interest and hoping to hold him more closely by having Paula there? I'm getting too old for intrigue, thought James in a sudden fit of revulsion, as he half-listened to Margaret telling Guy about the phone call and Emma's disappearance; all I want is for us to have a settled home together—Paula and me—and when she gets better.

'Do you agree, James?'

It was Margaret speaking, and he had to ask her to repeat the question.

'Don't you think it would be better if we all kept right away from the clinic for the time being?'

Her voice was brisk, almost peremptory. It was Guy's Margaret speaking, the woman who had chosen to marry a man considerably older than herself and to make him very dependent on her. It flashed through James's mind that he would hate to be married to a woman who organised him in this way, and he longed to force Margaret into being her real self, or what he believed to be her real self—puzzled and worried and relying on him for help.

But Guy was present, and he had to go along with her in front of Guy.

'You mean, we wait to see if anybody gets in touch with you?' He turned to Guy. 'What's your opinion? Do you think I ought

129

to keep out of this business now?'

He looked at Guy, but his words were directed at Margaret—a threat, a challenge, whatever way she liked to take them.

'I didn't say,' she began in a rather less commanding tone of volce.

Guy interrupted her. He spoke quietly, and it took James a second or two to realise that he was in fact very angry.

'In my opinion, which seems to count for less and less in this house, the whole matter ought to be put in the hands of the police.'

'But darling, there's no crime been committed,' said Margaret quickly. 'Except by James. Impersonation and abduction. I don't know how serious those offences are. Do you?' And she turned away from Guy and looked at James, challenging him, smiling at him.

This is intolerable, thought James, to be carrying on in Guy's presence the sort of love-hate relationship we seem to have established, and he wished with all his heart that he had never brought Paula here.

Guy was speaking again, in the same tense voice of suppressed fury and impatience.

'James can make a confession if he likes. It's his decision. I'm talking now of your suspicions that there is something criminal going on at the Windsor Clinic. It's up to the police to investigate, and I suggest—'

'But I haven't got any evidence,' protested

130

Margaret. 'They won't listen to me. They'll say I'm making it all up.'

'Are you?' demanded her husband. 'Or is it that you know your brother is deep in some illegal activity and you don't want to give him away?'

Margaret protested again. James had the feeling that this was not the first time there had been arguments of this nature, and it increased his growing suspicion that the relationship between the two of them was not exactly what Margaret had indicated. Guy was not, after all, the rather remote, self-centered, wife-protected intellectual, but a force to be reckoned with.

'I'd like to get away,' said James with determination. 'I have to go to my flat as well as Paula's. I've barely had time to glance at my mail since I got back from the States, let alone deal with any of it.'

This statement aroused a fellow feeling in Guy, as James had known it would.

'I wish I could offer to do some of these errands,' he said, 'but I'm sorry to say I've never learnt to drive a car.'

'That's all right, I don't mind,' said James. 'I'll just run up to Paula and get my instructions.'

He hurried out of the room, vaguely aware that Margaret was starting to say something, but determined to make his escape. But on the landing at the turn of the stairs he

131

hesitated, not knowing which room Paula was in; indeed, not knowing his way about the house except for the small room at the end of the corridor, where he and Margaret had talked and made love and finally slept a little in the early hours of the morning after her brother had gone.

Which of them had made the first move? Neither or both. At the time it had seemed right and inevitable in the circumstances. He didn't think Paula suspected anything, but even if she did, there was the unspoken agreement between them, had been for many years now, that both were free to have other relationships if they wished to. And the fact that in recent years they had become older and lazier and content with each other didn't alter this long-standing arrangement.

So Paula couldn't complain. But on the other hand James had a strong suspicion that she would be very hurt, all the more so if she knew that it wasn't just a very temporary impulse, but that he really did feel deeply stirred by Margaret Leeming, both repelled and attracted, fascinated and intrigued as he had not been for years by any other woman.

He must get out of this house and try to conquer this feeling. Action was what was needed, and a good dose of his ordinary daily life. His and Paula's.

He began to move up the short flight of stairs to the first floor, and it was here that

Margaret caught up with him.

'Guy's on the phone,' she said softly. 'One of his London calls just come through and it'll take a long time. He'll be better when he's immersed in his own affairs again, and I don't think we need trouble him anymore with the Windsor Clinic business.'

James said nothing. He felt more and more inclined to agree with Guy, but was determined not to argue with Margaret.

'Paula said,' she went on, 'that there was no need for you to ask her anything. She said you had the keys to her flat and would know what she needed.'

It was said in a most matter-of-fact way, but James could sense a whole weight of meaning behind it. Paula was staking out her prior claim on him, which meant that she must feel threatened, and Margaret knew it and was showing him how very discreet she herself could be. His longing to be away from the house became even stronger.

'All the same,' he said, 'I'll just look in on her before I go. I'd like to see how she is.'

'First door on the left at the top of the stairs,' said Margaret in the same noncommittal way, before she turned and went downstairs again.

James gave a very light tap on the door. There was no reply. He turned the handle and pushed it open as quietly as he could. Paula was fast asleep. She was lying on her

133

back, her arms sprawled over the white bedspread, and she was wearing a pale pink nightgown, a colour which normally she never wore. Her fair hair looked darker than usual against the white pillow and her face was very pale. But there was a calm relaxed air about her, and it seemed to be a peaceful sleep.

Sleep, the innocent sleep, thought James, his mind suddenly full of quotations from *Macbeth* down to W. H. Auden, and the sight of Paula at rest took away much of his own self-reproach. She would be safe and cared for here. But he certainly would bring along her favourite blue and white pyjamas and the kimono she had bought from the Hampstead Japanese shop, so that she would look more like herself and not so strange to him.

He let himself out of the room, taking great care not to disturb her, and ran down the stairs. From the half-open door of Guy's study came the sound of voices. It sounded as if he and Margaret were arguing again.

'Goodbye, I'll be back as soon as I can,' he called out, hoping to get out of the house without having to talk to either of them. But as he reached the front door he heard the phone ring, and it must have been for Guy because Margaret caught up with him as he was opening the door of his car.

'Paula's asleep,' he said before she could

134

speak. 'She looks better already. I can't tell you how grateful I am to you.'

'Paula's going to be fine,' said Margaret. 'It's you I'm worried about. My sixth sense tells me you are thinking of doing something rash.'

'I haven't time to,' replied James. 'I've got far too much to do.'

'Promise.' She put a hand on his arm.

'What do you want me to promise?'

They stared at each other in silence.

'I don't want you to take any risks,' said Margaret at last.

'I'm a careful driver, whatever Paula may say,' said James with a forced smile.

'You know I don't mean that.'

'All right. I'm going to phone the clinic and say that Paula is with friends. They've probably started a police search already, and we want to shut that one up.'

'Yes, you'd better do that.'

Margaret looked as if she was about to say something more, but thought better of it. James's normal open and lively manner had been succeeded by a sort of closed obstinacy that would be very difficult to break down. Paula knew that look well and always left him alone at such times.

'Goodbye, good luck,' said Margaret. 'See you this evening.'

CHAPTER ELEVEN

Windsor Clinic first, decided James. He was in the mood for action and confrontation. Margaret Leeming had that sort of effect on him. Challenge and stimulation. But did he really want that at his time of life? It was probably just a symptom of approaching middle-age, a grasping after lost youth.

Middle-aged lecturers were notoriously prone to fall for glamorous young students.

But Margaret wasn't young and glamorous. She was middle-aged herself and the sort of woman who improved with age. All the way back to London he could not stop thinking about her, and only when he was actually looking for a parking place near the front entrance of the clinic was he able to pull his thoughts into the direction of his present errand.

Matron's office first. Then just tell the truth. Paula didn't want to go with Mr. Easebourne to the convalescent home, and had begged James to take her away at once. She was not a prisoner; she had every right to discharge herself if she wanted to. He had made other arrangements for her care during convalescence.

And so on. All very straightforward and reasonable. Almost disappointingly so. He was spoiling for a fight but it looked as if he might be denied it.

The sight of Jack Easebourne's white Mercedes in the driveway cheered him up. Parked beyond it was a police car.

James pushed through the swing doors, waved at the receptionist, and crossed to the matron's office. The door was half open, and from beyond it came the sound of many voices.

The receptionist was calling to him. He took no notice of her, but gave a perfunctory knock on the half-open door and walked in. There was a sudden silence. James had the feeling of being stared at by at least half a dozen pairs of eyes, and then a woman's voice, low but clear, called out, 'That's the man! That's the one who abducted my patient after pretending to be her husband.'

The voice came from near the window, the other side of the matron's desk. James looked across and saw a strikingly handsome face which seemed familiar, but for the moment he couldn't put a name to it. Rachel Feverel, he finally said to himself, the matron at Heath House, and he turned to the senior of the two policemen who were standing near to the door.

'There's a perfectly simple explanation,' he began, in what was intended to be a friendly yet authoritative manner but which actually sounded rather supercilious, 'my friend and colleague Dr. Paula Glenning—'

'Whom you spirited away this morning,' interrupted Mrs. Kennedy.

'This joker seems to be in the habit of abducting patients from nursing-homes,' said the man James had seen the day before, whom he took to be Jack Easebourne. He was perched on the edge of Mrs. Kennedy's desk and succeeded in sounding even more offensively superior than James himself.

'As you seem to be making a habit of maltreating your patients,' said James, finding himself suddenly violently angry and making no attempt whatever to hide it.

'If you gentlemen,' began the police sergeant with an air of resignation, 'would allow me to ask—'

'That's an appalling thing to say!' cried Mrs. Kennedy, going very red in the face. 'If you are suggesting, Mr. Goff, that—'

'I'm suggesting that both Mrs. Leeming and Mrs. Glenning have been given overdoses of drugs in order to induce states of mental confusion,' said James loudly and clearly.

'If you have any evidence, sir,' the police sergeant tried again, 'then perhaps you will—'

'I've got evidence in the case of Mrs. Leeming,' interrupted James. 'She held back some of the tablets because she's a nurse herself and she suspected she was being overdosed, and I got the tablets analysed and can give you all the particulars, Officer.'

The police sergeant, a tired-looking middle-aged man, looked as if he would like nothing better than to walk out of the room, but he said resignedly, 'All right. If you would like to make a statement, Mr. Goff, and I need hardly remind you that to accuse professional people of serious misconduct is not a matter to be undertaken lightly.'

James was not listening. He was looking at Mr. Jack Easebourne and Mrs. Jenny Kennedy, who were glaring at each other, the man very pale, the woman more flushed than ever. And then he glanced across to where Rachel Feverel stood by the window. She was looking at them too, and it was impossible to guess what she was thinking.

'I fully realise that it is a very serious accusation to make,' said James to the sergeant, 'but as I say, I can bring supporting evidence, and in view of the fact that I myself have been accused of a criminal offence, I should like to explain the exact circumstances in order to clear myself of any criminal intent.'

The sergeant nodded to the police constable, who produced a pen and a notebook. 'Is there anywhere we can go without being disturbed?' he asked Mrs. Kennedy.

'Yes,' replied the matron. 'Room 10 is

unoccupied since Mrs. Glenning left. It's on the ground floor. Turn right and it is on the left at the far end of the corridor. Mr. Goff will show you.'

'Now just a minute,' Jack Easebourne addressed the sergeant. 'I hope you realise, Officer, that complaints made by lay people against the medical profession can only rightly be assessed by other members of the profession, and that there are in fact proper channels for the investigation of such complaints. In other words, this is not a police matter at all.'

'Yes sir, I quite appreciate that,' replied the sergeant wearily, 'but since I have been called in to hear an accusation made against this gentleman here, it is in order for me to hear his own statement on the matter.'

James was again looking at the surgeon and at the matron of the Windsor Clinic, and saying to himself, She's the one who called in the police—she's torn in two, Jenny Kennedy. She hasn't completely lost hopes of becoming Mrs. Easebourne the third or fourth, but she's eaten up with jealousy of the glamorous Rachel. She's in a mess, and her Jack is scared of what she will do next. What about Rachel? What's her aim in all this?

'... medical profession must be represented while Mr. Goff is making his statement,' Jack Easebourne was saying in a

140

very determined manner.

James would have liked to retort, but was not too sure of his ground. It was quite true that complaints about medical treatment should be made through the proper channels, and by the patient in question. And there was also no doubt that there would be expert evidence in plenty to justify the treatment meted out to Margaret and to Paula. He couldn't possibly, on his own, prove that there had been any misconduct.

His own fury was beginning to subside and something like caution to take over. There was an accusation of impersonation and abduction to answer. He had better get on with it now, and only bring in the counter-accusation insofar as it was necessary to justify his own actions.

'Perhaps Mr. Easebourne would like to be present himself while I make my statement,' he said smoothly.

'Thank you,' Jack sneered, 'but I doubt if that would be in order.'

The sergeant, on his way out of the room, ignored this. 'Did you say Room 10?' he asked Mrs. Kennedy.

James answered. 'Yes, I'll show you the way.'

The sergeant turned to the constable, who was about to follow them. 'No need to come too. You can wait here.'

'Just a minute.' Jack Easebourne's voice

was loud and clear as he addressed the police sergeant and deliberately avoided looking at James. 'I think you ought to know that on two occasions Mrs. Leeming has herself been a patient—not in this clinic but in another one—suffering from psychotic symptoms which included hallucinations and what is commonly known as persecution mania.'

As he spoke these last words he turned to face James, who congratulated himself on showing no reaction.

'Thank you, sir,' said the sergeant resignedly. 'We will take note of it,' and he stepped back to allow James to lead the way.

Room 10 had been cleaned and tidied, the bed re-made, and the flower vases removed. James sat down on the edge of the bed, absorbing the shock of Jack Easebourne's last words. And yet they were not entirely a shock because in some way he had known this all along; he had allowed his own suspicions to be overwhelmed by Paula's certainties and by his own dislike and suspicion of the Windsor Clinic and all its works.

Not to mention the fascination that Margaret had for him.

'Did you know, Mr. Goff,' enquired the sergeant as he seated himself on the chair next to the bed, 'that Mrs. Leeming had suffered from persecution mania?'

'Not for sure,' replied James, 'but I had

142

grasped as much.' Then he went on, playing for time so that he could readjust his ideas before making his statement. 'Would you say that it was in order to publicise a patient's medical history in such a way?'

'I don't know anything about medical etiquette,' replied the sergeant with distaste, 'but the statement has to be taken into account.'

'Of course it has,' James readily agreed. 'And although, not being an expert, I didn't know for certain, I've been taking this possibility into account all along. So has my friend and colleague, Dr. Glenning.'

Rapidly reforming his ideas as he spoke, James told his story. Professor Leeming became the centre of it. In James's most persuasive tones, Guy changed from being a respected acquaintance into a close personal friend.

'He was very worried that he couldn't get home any sooner,' said James after explaining how he and Guy had talked about Margaret when they were at the convention in Washington, 'particularly in view of this weakness of his wife's, and extremely anxious that she should be brought home at once to be in the care of the doctor who knows and understands her condition.'

James paused for a moment, searching his memory. Presumably the others had already given the sergeant their version of events.

Was he saying anything that would conflict with their evidence? Not with Rachel Feverel's, certainly, and as for Jack Easebourne, James had never met him until today. Mrs. Kennedy was the only one he had actually spoken to at some length, when he had told her he would meet Professor Leeming at the airport.

'To save Professor Leeming from going to London and then back to Sussex to collect his wife,' James went on, 'we'd decided to go together to the nursing-home where Mrs. Leeming had been taken. But the flight was delayed and it was getting late. I made a quick decision—perhaps I ought not to have done so, but at the time it seemed to me the best thing to do—to fetch Mrs. Leeming myself, and on the way it occurred to me that there might be some difficulty in explaining my credentials and that it would be much the simplest if instead of acting on behalf of Professor Leeming, I actually presented myself as him.'

He paused. The sergeant nodded noncommittally.

'Margaret—Mrs. Leeming—was very glad indeed to see me,' went on James. 'The nursing-home appeared to be of a most luxurious nature, and no doubt the treatment she was receiving could be justified by medical necessity in most cases, but her case was rather different. She wanted to be at home, and her husband wanted her to be at home so that he could take over the full responsibility for her care. It was in these circumstances that I took her away, against the advice of the matron. If I have committed an offence against the law, then obviously I shall have to pay the penalty.'

James paused, wondering what impression he was making. The police sergeant's face was quite impassive.

'This professor,' he said at last, 'what is his phone number and address?'

James gave them. Surely Guy would bear out his story? Surely. After all, if it hadn't been for James's action, Guy would have arrived home to find no wife and would himself have had to get her out of the clutches of...

Or would he? How much did Guy really care what happened to Margaret? If all he had wanted was a good housekeeper ... On the other hand, suppose he really cared for her, suppose he was jealous of any other man who attracted her interest?

The police sergeant was speaking again. 'This business of a possible maltreatment—do you want to pursue it any further?'

After the very briefest of hesitations James said, with an air of taking the sergeant into his confidence, 'I honestly don't know. Personally I'm quite sure that there's been

145

some sort of irregularity, to put it mildly, but whether there's any point in taking on the medical establishment is another matter. You know how they stick together. Unless they've actually killed somebody or performed the wrong operation.'

James paused a moment, then added, 'What do you think yourself? D'you think it's worth pursuing?'

'It's entirely up to you, sir,' said the sergeant.

'Okay. Let's drop it. Do you want to check up on me now? With Professor Leeming, I mean. I've got a lot of business to attend to and the sooner I can get away the better.'

The sergeant got up and moved towards the telephone.

'Dial 9–1 for an outside line,' said James. 'Do you want me to go?'

'Yes, please.'

'I suppose I'd better go back to Matron's office.'

A faint smile appeared on the policeman's face. 'You might prefer to wait in the corridor. I shan't be long.'

James, somewhat reassured by this evidence that the sergeant was, after all, human, left the room and walked a few yards along the corridor. It was a relief to be alone, not having to keep up any pretence, and to have a chance really to take in the fact that Margaret Leeming had in the past been treated for delusions of persecution.

Of course James had only Jack Easebourne's word for this, and he had no faith in the surgeon's honesty, but it seemed unlikely that he would make a statement that could easily be disproved. On the other hand, Jack attended patients at other clinics than the Windsor. Wasn't it possible that he himself had been treating Margaret during these 'paranoid' episodes? Or if not actually treating, for surely it was not the business of a surgeon to meddle in psychiatry, couldn't he have been in league with matrons or nurses who had given Margaret drugs that created such delusions?

I'm getting as bad as Paula, said James to himself, trying to get a grip on his roaming thoughts; let's stick to the immediate problem: are they going to charge me with abduction or whatever, and what is Guy saying about me now?

As if in answer to this question, the door of Room 10 opened and the lugubrious police sergeant emerged.

'Professor Leeming was very helpful,' he said, 'but I shall have to find out whether anybody wants to make a charge—There's no need for you to wait if you're in a hurry to get away.'

'I'd rather wait,' said James as they walked along the corridor together. 'I'd like to get this matter cleared up straight away. I'll be

147

waiting at Reception.'

The door of the matron's office closed behind the sergeant. James hesitated for a moment, wondering whether to stay there and try to hear what was being said, but the sight of a nurse coming along the corridor that led to Room 10 caused him to change his mind. She was a dark, sturdy-looking girl and the face looked familiar. As she came nearer he stepped forward to greet her.

'Louise!'

She stopped suddenly, nearly dropping the tray she was carrying.

'Mr. Goff—oh, I'm so glad to see you! How's Paula? What's happened? You can't think how worried I've been about her.'

'She's fine. I've taken her to some friends of ours who'll look after her well. Look, we can't talk now—you're busy and I've got to go in a minute. When do you go off duty?'

'Four-thirty.'

'Are you free then?'

'I can be.'

'I'll be at my flat—here's the address—it's only five minutes away. See you between four-thirty and five. Okay?'

'I'll be there. You're quite sure Paula—'

'Absolutely sure.' James spoke with far more conviction than he really felt. The thought that he might have made a serious mistake in leaving Paula under Margaret's care was nagging at him more and more.

'Tell you all about it then. Look—we'd better not be seen talking. See you.'

The door of the matron's office was opening. 'See you,' echoed Louise, and hurried away.

James moved quickly to the reception area, sat down, picked up a newspaper, and hid his face behind it. He could hear the receptionist talking on the phone. She was young and lively, and she was obviously not making a business call.

'Can't stop now,' she said. 'They're all coming out. Tell you this evening. It's not the first time they've had the police here ... 'bye now. Kisses.'

Instinctively James lowered his newspaper. At the same moment the girl looked up from her desk and glanced in his direction. They smiled at each other. If I had five minutes, thought James, I'd get her to tell me what she knows.

He raised the newspaper hurriedly again as the voices and footsteps came nearer. Only when he heard the matron asking impatiently where Mr. Goff was, did he come out from behind the cover of the paper.

'Well, have you decided on my fate?'

James stood up as he spoke, looking first at the matron and then at the police sergeant.

The latter answered. 'No charge is to be made, sir. Thank you for your co operation.'

'Thank you, ' said James. 'I'll be off then.'

'Just a minute,' said the matron.

James turned back reluctantly. Was he to be summoned to some sort of private bargaining session? And if so, was there anything to be learned from it? He was longing to get away and sort out his ideas at leisure, but it would be a pity to miss a clue.

It was at this moment that he first admitted to himself that he didn't care whether or not the Windsor Clinic was the centre of some sort of criminal activity. The mystery that was nagging at him incessantly was that of Margaret Leeming herself, and if anybody other than Margaret knew the answer, surely that person would be Jack Easebourne.

'I won't keep you a moment,' Mrs. Kennedy was saying. 'It's only to give you the things Mrs. Glenning left behind. I take it that you will be seeing her?'

'Yes. Thank you,' said James. For a moment he had almost forgotten Paula's existence. 'Thanks,' he said again as he took the bag from Mrs. Kennedy. It was alarming that he had, even for a very short while, ceased to be concerned about Paula because he had become so obsessed with another woman. 'I'm going on to Mrs. Glenning's apartment now,' he added unnecessarily, 'to collect her mail for her.'

'The medical records,' said the matron very stiffly, 'will of course be available to

150

whoever is taking over the case.'

James thanked her again and made his escape. In the midst of his own preoccupations, it did occur to him to wonder how Jack was coping with these two formidable ladies, both of whom appeared to have designs on him and to be bitterly jealous of each other. He himself, James Goff, had in his younger days been in a similar position, and had not come out of it with much dignity.

He smiled at the recollection. When he had told Paula about it she had laughed too. What a friend and companion Paula was. Not a scrap of jealousy in her make-up. A great wave of sentiment swept over him as he got into his car. But almost immediately he thought that if it hadn't been for Paula he would never have known Margaret at all. And the next minute he was telling himself that it was only because Paula was sick that he had snatched at the first woman who became available. As simple as that.

Except that it wasn't so simple. If it had been, there would be none of this constantly nagging guilt and doubt.

CHAPTER TWELVE

So deeply engaged was James in his struggle of conscience that he almost forgot his next errand. It was the sight of a young girl taking a dog for a walk that reminded him of it.

Emma.

Judging by the conversation that James had overheard between Margaret and her brother, Emma's father had definitely been involved in illegal activities, and Margaret, as well as Emma's mother, had known about them for some time.

This, surely, must be true and not part of some paranoid delusion of Margaret's. Tony had admitted it himself, and had blamed Jack for involving him unwittingly in the business of laundering money from the profits of drug-dealing.

It rather looked as if Guy might know about it too, and that he disapproved of Margaret supporting her brother. But surely, if Margaret had indeed been protecting Tony, it could only be for Emma's sake.

Almost with reluctance, James found his thoughts swinging back again to sympathy and even admiration for Margaret. At any rate, he said to himself, as he parked the car outside a large old brick mansion that had been converted into separate apartments,

Emma herself is completely innocent and may well be at risk; and I myself promised her that she could call on me at any time if she needed help.

The Fieldings lived on the ground floor. James rang the bell three times and was disappointed, but hardly surprised, that there was no response. After a moment's thought, he made his way down to the basement and rang the bell at a wooden door that needed repairing and repainting. So did the window, shut and barred, that was a few feet away from the door.

James noted the shabbiness while he tried to remember the name of Emma's friend. Something beginning with J. Janice? Jacinth?

A voice came from behind the door. 'Who's that?'

It was a child's voice, sharp and wary but not afraid. James knew that he was being looked at through the eyehole in the centre of the door.

'I'm James Goff, a friend of Emma's,' he replied. 'Is she with you?'

'Can you give me any proof of identity?'

The voice sounded very adult, but the child could scarcely be much older than Emma herself.

'Here's my card,' replied James. 'I'm shoving it under the door.'

There was a short pause, then the voice said, 'You could easily have got hold of a card. How about your driving licence?'

'I can't push it through,' said James. 'It's too thick.'

'We had to board up our letter-box,' explained the voice. 'I'll put the chain on and open. You sound all right.'

The door was opened a couple of inches and James put his driving licence into the small hand that appeared round it.

Half a minute later the chain was removed and the door opened. 'I'm sorry, Mr. Goff,' said the girl. 'You see, we have to be very careful. My mother is white but my father comes from India. He's left us and Mother is out at her job.'

'Yes, I see. Jasmine,' said James, suddenly remembering the name. 'I'm sorry to disturb you but I wondered if Emma was with you. Her Aunt Margaret wants to know. So do I. I don't know whether Emma has told you—'

'I know all about it,' interrupted Jasmine. 'Would you like to come in?'

She held the door open for him, then shut it and replaced the chain. She was rather taller than Emma, with a beautiful complexion slightly darker than European, dark brown eyes, and long black hair tied with a white ribbon.

James followed her into a room containing a large table, chairs, lots of books, and a guitar.

'I'm interrupting your studies,' he said. 'I

won't be long. It's only to know about Emma.'

'She's not here,' replied Jasmine, 'but she left me a note.' From under a book lying on the table she extracted a folded piece of paper. 'Would you like to read it?'

'"I have to go with Dad,"' read James. '"He's running away and I have to keep watch on him in case he does anything silly. I'll phone you as soon as I can. Lots of love and thanks to you and your Mum from Emma."'

The handwriting was round and upright, firm and clear.

'Did you know Emma's mother?' asked James as he handed the note back to Jasmine.

'Not very well,' replied the child. 'She was often ill and she had to go away.'

'Go away? You mean for a holiday?'

'They said for a holiday, but Emma thought it was some sort of clinic. She had nervous breakdowns. That's what Emma said, but her father pretended she was just having a rest.'

'I see,' said James, remembering his talk with Margaret about her sister-in-law.

'Was she taking drugs?' he asked Jasmine, deciding that the children knew so much that it was useless to try to pretend to them.

'I think so,' replied the dark girl.

'Hard drugs—heroin, cocaine—not just

155

prescribed tranquillisers?'

'Emma wasn't sure,' was the reply. 'Emma's mother was sometimes very sleepy, but it might have been the tranquillisers.'

'And who gave them to her? Who was her doctor?'

'Emma thought it was a friend of her father who often came to see them. He's a consultant surgeon.'

'I see,' said James thoughtfully, and was silent for a moment, digesting this information.

'Sometimes she went to stay with Emma's Auntie Margaret,' continued the child.

'In Sussex?'

'No. Emma's auntie wasn't married then. She had a flat in London somewhere. I don't know where. And I don't know where Emma is now and I'm so scared for her.'

Jasmine had been answering the questions with such composure that James was quite surprised to hear her voice turning into that of a frightened child.

'Look, Jasmine,' he said, sitting down at the big table. 'I don't know where Emma is either, but I'm quite sure she is all right. That's one thing that is quite certain— Emma's father won't let any harm come to her. Whatever he has done, there's no doubt that he loves Emma very much. That's true, isn't it?'

'Yes, but—'

156

James waited. 'But what?' he said at last.

'He might do something silly. Emma says so.'

'He's already been doing something very silly,' said James. 'He's been handling drugs profits, and it's possible that he's been found out and is running away. He will have known that this could happen one day and he'll have made some arrangements. He may be planning to go abroad, but whatever it is, he won't let any harm come to Emma. You have to believe that, Jasmine. I believe it. Don't you?'

The child looked happier. Much older and more experienced people than she had been convinced by James's most persuasive manner.

'What time does your mother get home?' he asked.

'Half past five.'

'And I've got to go in a minute or two. I've got someone coming to see me. Do you mind being here alone?'

The dark girl shrugged. 'I'm used to it. It's Mum who worries about me. But it was nice having Emma.'

James stood up. 'You'll have her back again. And she will get in touch. And I'll be in touch too, if I may.'

They walked towards the door.

'What shall I say if the police come asking about Emma's father?' asked Jasmine. 'Shall

157

I show them the note?'

James thought for a moment. 'What do you think yourself?'

'I'd rather not.'

'You could throw it away. Burn it.'

'But it might be the last—I mean, suppose something's happened to Emma—and it's in her writing, and Emma's my friend. Suppose I don't ever see her again!'

'Of course you're going to see her again. How about you giving me the letter to take care of? Then if the police ask if she left any message you can truthfully say you haven't got one, and your mother can say that too.'

'All right,' said Jasmine, controlling her agitation and handing over the piece of paper. 'I'll do that.'

'And they probably won't come at all. What are you reading?' James leant over the open book that lay on the table. *How We Learnt to Count and Calculate*. A history of mathematics. This looks rather fun. And I see you play chess. Does Emma?'

'I'm teaching her.'

'Good luck to you both.'

With renewed reassurances, James took himself off. Emma's friend had put some quite new ideas into his mind, and he longed to question her further about Emma's mother and Emma's Auntie Margaret, but decided that the child was suffering quite enough strain already. Any further questions must wait until the mother was at home. Besides, he had an appointment with Paula's nurse, Louise, from whom he had hopes of further revelations.

Louise was walking up to the entrance of the apartment block as James turned his car into the drive. The phone was ringing as they came into his flat. He hurried to it, his mind suddenly full of fears for Paula, listened a moment, and then visibly relaxed.

'That was my neighbours.' He turned to Louise. 'They look after my cat when I'm away and she's with them now. They saw me come in and thought I might wonder where Rosie was.'

'I've never met a cat called Rosie,' said Louise.

'Ah, thereby hangs a tale. Paula will tell you about it some day. I'm going to make some tea—or would you prefer coffee?'

'Tea, please.'

When James had brought it, Louise said, 'I've been worrying all afternoon about Paula. I knew something was wrong when Matron told me not to come in this morning, and when I found that Paula had been given creozepam—'

'The same as Mrs. Leeming,' broke in James. 'How did you know?'

'It's being prescribed, legitimately, for two other patients,' replied Louise. 'We have to keep a full record of the condition of each

159

patient, including medication given, and as soon as we come on duty the first job is to read through it. There was a note in the writing of one of the agency nurses, and I managed to speak to her before she left and ask about Paula, and she said that Paula had been taken to a convalescent home by Mr. Easebourne and that Matron was in a vile mood. After that I was too busy to find out any more until the police turned up just as I was coming through Reception and I spoke to Geraldine, who was at the desk, and she told me Paula had been spirited away by a tall dark man and they were determined to get him. I guessed it was you, and I asked Geraldine to tell me all she knew, but her story was rather garbled, so it's over to you now.'

James quickly explained. 'Paula only took one of the pills. She got suspicious and managed to hide the others. And we got out through the gap in the hedge to the next-door garden.'

Louise smiled. 'Well done, James Bond.' Then she quickly became serious again. 'Where is Paula now? You said she was with some friends.'

'Yes. The wife's a trained nurse.'

James suddenly found himself reluctant to mention Margaret by name, and hoped that this would satisfy Louise, but of course it didn't.

'If you'll give me the name and address I'll go and see Paula myself,' she said. 'I've looked after her since the op. and I think she'd like to see me.' She paused a moment but James, becoming ever more doubtful and reluctant to mention the Leemings, made no comment.

'Besides,' went on Louise, 'I think I can fix up for her to see the surgeon who was supposed to do the op. Miss Twigg. She's back at work now and is coming to see her patients at the Windsor Clinic tomorrow. So if you could tell me—'

She waited for the reply, which James could no longer avoid giving; after he had told her, she exclaimed in disapproving surprise, 'What on earth did you do that for?'

'Because Guy Leeming is a friend of mine—and I wanted to get Paula right out of London, and I knew Margaret would look after her. She's very grateful to Paula and to me and is very pleased to do something in return.'

'So Margaret suggested it,' said Louise, more as a statement than as a question. 'I thought as much.'

James did not immediately respond. He was thinking back, trying to remember. Had it really been Margaret who initiated the whole idea? Had he really been so easily manipulated?

'Why shouldn't the Leemings look after

161

Paula?' he said at last. 'I wish you'd tell me, Louise.'

'Professor Leeming may be all right,' was the grudging reply. 'I've never met him. But if, as I suspect, his wife can twist him round her little finger—'

'She can't,' broke in James. 'He's got a mind of his own.'

'I'm glad to hear it. But I still wish—'

'Why don't you trust Margaret Leeming?' demanded James.

'Because she's mentally unstable. Paranoid.'

'She has good reason to be,' snapped James.

'I don't mean this recent business. I mean in the past.'

'Perhaps somebody was trying to make her appear so.'

'It's not impossible,' admitted Louise, 'but all the same I don't feel happy about Paula being there. Whether Mrs. Leeming is unbalanced or not, she is the sort of person who gets into difficult situations and drags other people into them too.'

'You're right about that,' said James with feeling. 'And Paula's the sort of person who lets herself be dragged. Look, let's not argue about this. The only thing that matters is for Paula to get well. Do you think I ought to take her somewhere else?'

'There's another nursing-home where

Miss Twigg has patients,' said Louise thoughtfully, 'but it's even more expensive than the Windsor.'

'That doesn't matter. What's your opinion—medically, I mean?'

'I think,' said Louise after a short pause, 'that it's obviously not good for Paula to keep being moved. On the other hand she does love to know what's going on. Why don't you let her decide for herself?'

'You mean I should tell her that the woman who is nursing her is not to be trusted?'

'I didn't say that!' cried Louise. She got up and moved impatiently about James's living-room, which was not very easy, since the room was crowded with bookcases and good old pieces of furniture too big for a modern flat.

'Then what exactly do you mean? What precisely have you got against Margaret Leeming?'

James was trying to speak as if he had no personal interest in Margaret, but he could tell by Louise's reaction that he had not succeeded. She looked at him keenly and said, 'Personally I rather like Margaret, and I don't think she's dangerously unbalanced— not schizophrenic or anything like that. But I know she manipulates people—she's such a good actress that they believe her, and I don't think she's always quite clear herself

163

about where truth ends and fantasy begins.'

James did not reply, but his mind went back to Emma talking about how her mother and her Aunt Margaret loved 'pretending,' and how her aunt always won in the end.

'Is it true that she had an affair with Jack Easebourne?' he asked.

'I think so. And there have been others.' Louise, who had been staring at the carpet, glanced up at James enquiringly.

'It's none of my business,' she added, 'and I don't care what either of them does, but I do care about Paula and I'm afraid Margaret could make trouble between you and Paula.'

'I see,' said James coolly.

'That's none of my business either.' Louise was beginning to sound embarrassed, unsure of herself. 'I don't think I'd better say any more.' She moved towards the door. 'I'll go now. And if there's anything I can do—'

'You might as well give me the address of this other nursing-home where Miss Twigg sees patients,' said James.

When this was done he said, 'Do you know anything about Margaret's brother, Tony Fielding?'

'I don't know him well and I don't think I'll repeat gossip.'

'And his wife? Did you ever meet her?'

'Once. She was very pretty and lively. Much too good for him.'

'Did she kill herself?'

164

'The coroner decided the drug-overdose was accidental. I must go now. Give my love to Paula. Goodbye.'

She was gone, and James was left to curse himself for having bungled this interview from which he had hoped to gain a lot, and then to blame Margaret for having taken such a grip on him that she had upset his usual self-control. Louise had said she feared that Margaret would come between himself and Paula. Wasn't that exactly what he was afraid of himself?

An overwhelming desire to hear Paula's voice seized him, and he sat down at his desk pulling the telephone towards him.

CHAPTER THIRTEEN

Guy Leeming, sitting at his desk reading yet another request for a reference for one of his former students, lifted the telephone and spoke resignedly.

'Yes?'

'Sorry to disturb you,' said James. 'I really wanted to speak to Paula. Is she all right?'

'As far as I know, yes. Margaret's looking after her. I'll put you through to Margaret. Hold on.'

But I don't want to speak to Margaret, thought James irritably; I only want to speak

165

to Paula. What can I say—invent something quickly—that makes it imperative that I speak to Paula?

Margaret's voice came over the line, very calm and confident.

'I'm in Paula's flat,' lied James, 'collecting her mail. There are one or two urgent things that I can deal with for her, but I must speak to her first. Could you put me through?'

'Is it absolutely essential?' countered Margaret. 'Paula ate some lunch and she's fast asleep now. She badly needs rest and I'd much rather not wake her. Can't it wait until you get back here?'

'I suppose it can,' said James feebly.

'When do you expect to come?'

'I haven't much more to do. I ought to be with you about half past seven.'

'Good. I'll make dinner for eight o'clock. With luck Paula will be able to join us. I'm making up your bed again in the little room. You won't want to drive to London yet again tonight.'

'No, I certainly won't. Thanks,' said James with the sensation of sinking more and more deeply into quicksands of his own making.

*   *   *

Paula was sitting in her room in the armchair by the window, turning the pages of a fashion magazine in a dreamy manner. She had bathed and dressed in a cotton frock of Margaret's that was comfortably too big for her. The bed was made, there were yellow roses on the dressing-table, and physically she felt more comfortable than she had at any time since the operation.

It was very easy to relax and allow her weakened body to determine her needs and her thoughts and her expectations.

I need some new clothes, she said to herself; I'll treat myself to a visit to Harrods when I can get about again. But the next moment her mind had jumped to James. What was he doing now? Collecting things from her flat? Or investigating on his own? She did not believe his promise that he was not going anywhere near the Windsor Clinic. He'd know that she would be longing to learn what was happening, and if all their years of love and friendship meant anything at all, he would do his best to find out for her; not to mention the satisfying of his own curiosity, which was greater than he would ever admit.

There was a knock on the door and Margaret came in carrying a tray with tea. Paula looked up and smiled her thanks.

'But you oughtn't to be doing so much running about for me,' she added.

'I'm only doing the essentials,' replied Margaret. 'Lifting or dragging things is something you'll have to avoid for quite a long time.'

'Yes, I'm beginning to realise that,' said Paula.

If I think of her purely as a nurse, she was saying to herself, then I feel at ease with her; but if I think of her as a mystery, or even worse, as a woman who fascinates James, then I can't come to terms with her at all and I wish with all my heart that I'd never taken any notice of the patient in the next room to me at the clinic.

The medical conversation came to an end, and Paula, feeling that she ought to say something, came out with what was uppermost in her mind.

'I wonder how James is getting on.'

She had been determined not to mention him to Margaret, but as so often happens when one is ill at ease, she said the very thing she didn't want to.

'I don't know,' said Margaret placidly, 'but I expect he will tell us all about it at dinner.'

'Yes, I expect so.' Paula meekly accepted the implication that she had no greater claim on James's attention than had Margaret or Guy. 'Actually I half expected him to telephone.'

Margaret shook her head. 'No call, but I'll tell you who I have heard from, which has been a great relief to me, and I know you'll be glad too to hear that Emma is all right.

Tony phoned—I don't know where from—to say that he and Emma are having a holiday until it's safe to come back.'

'In case he gets caught for laundering drugs profits, I suppose,' said Paula.

'How did you know?'

There was a sharpness in Margaret's voice which had not been there before.

'James told me when we drove down here this morning,' replied Paula.

'I see.'

There followed a silence, but this time Paula did not feel under any obligation to break it.

Margaret sat down and poured herself some tea before she spoke again. 'I'm sure there's no need to ask you to keep this to yourself. Tony has been very foolish, and I won't attempt to defend him except to add that he was acting under pressure.'

'I'm sorry I mentioned it,' said Paula. 'Of course I shall keep it to myself.'

She was about to add that James could also be relied on to keep quiet, but changed her mind. Much better not to mention James when talking to Margaret. They would only provoke each other. Try to remember Margaret as the patient next door, frightened and feeling herself threatened because she knew too much.

'Margaret,' she said impulsively, 'do you believe it was your brother who was behind

169

this attempt to drug you so much that you got confused?'

'I don't know,' said Margaret after a brief hesitation. 'It's more likely that Jack was behind it.'

'But if they've been involved in this drug business for years—I mean, when did you find out?'

Again some hesitation. 'I'd suspected for a long time, but it wasn't until after the accident—Jack and Tony were in my room at the clinic. They thought I wasn't conscious, but I was. They said something that confirmed my suspicions and later I went and gave away that I'd heard them. Presumably that's what decided Jack to try to keep me quiet or to make my evidence worthless. But he needn't have bothered. As if I would ever give Tony away! He's an idiot, but he's the only relative I've got left, and he's Emma's father.'

'I see,' said Paula thoughtfully. 'So you did know, all along, but when we talked in the clinic you said you didn't know what it was all about and why they should be doping you.'

'Because I didn't want anybody to know about Tony,' said Margaret almost too glibly.

'No, of course you didn't. And there was no reason why you should trust me. No, I won't have any more tea, thanks.'

Margaret stood up. 'You're getting tired. I'll leave you in peace till dinner time.'

'I'm going to lie down again now,' said Paula, glad to revert once more to the nurse-patient relationship.

After Margaret had gone, she did indeed relax on the bed. The feeling of physical ease was still strong within her, but the dreaminess had gone and her mind was working sharply and clearly.

Margaret wanted James. That was quite clear. Whether as a permanent proposition or only a short-term relationship, Paula could not guess. Perhaps Margaret didn't even know that herself, and certainly she would be unwise to give up the comfort and security of her life with Guy without a very definite commitment on the part of James. But nevertheless the pursuit of James was more important to Margaret at the moment than even Emma's well-being was, and certainly more important than her brother, or Jack Easebourne, or anybody else connected with the Windsor Clinic. As for Guy, presumably he could be fitted in somehow or other, and kept in ignorance. Maybe something similar had already happened in their marriage.

Therefore Paula, with her prior claim on James, must be the chief obstacle.

And my own chief aim, said Paula to herself, is to hold on to James, and to do that

I must understand why Margaret has such a fascination for him.

She lay and thought about this for quite a while, remembering the women who had attracted him over the years, and came to the conclusion that a lot of Margaret Leeming's appeal for him must lie in the air of mystery which surrounded her. In this respect she was like the girl he had once wanted to marry.

James was bored with the obvious and the predictable. Remove the mystery and much of the attraction would vanish as well. So what is my own hold on him, Paula asked herself. Certainly not mystery, not after all these years. But after a moment's reflection she decided that perhaps it was just that. Paula's own love of mysteries, and her determination to get to the bottom of them, provided James with a sort of vicarious satisfaction for his own wishes.

Paula smiled to herself at her own line of reasoning. If this was true, then she had better make sure she never lost her inquisitiveness. Suddenly there came into her mind a picture of James and herself, old and grey, plodding slowly and rheumatically after a young woman whose strange behaviour had stimulated their curiosity, and she laughed aloud.

CHAPTER FOURTEEN

James pushed his telephone away and leaned back in his chair, staring across the desk and out of the window. The lawn surrounding the apartment block sloped downwards to a brick wall, beyond which he could see the familiar view of Hampstead Heath. The grassy slopes were worn and yellowed from the passing of many footsteps during this exceptionally dry summer, and the trees looked thirsty too.

On this side of the apartment block the sound of London rush-hour traffic was muted, the afternoon was hot, and James was very weary. Hampstead Heath dissolved into a dream, and he came back to consciousness to find something soft and warm brushing against his face.

'Rosie!' He raised a hand to stroke the little black cat who was perched on his shoulder. 'I'm neglecting you dreadfully. You can have some milk and some biscuits and then you'll have to go back next door. Do you want to use your own door or shall I take you round?'

By the time James had made arrangements for Rosie and packed an overnight case for himself, another half hour had passed. He would have to hurry to be with the Leemings in time for an eight o'clock dinner, and he had not yet been to Paula's flat.

The anxiety about Paula had somewhat receded. With Guy in the house, he told himself, there was really no harm that could come to her. Paula wasn't completely helpless, and she certainly would not swallow any tablets that she was not quite sure about. He must go and fetch her letters, and he would very much like to speak to Emma's friends again. Jasmine's mother must surely be home by now.

Still undecided, James got into his car, turned it round, and waited at the front gate for a chance to join the stream of traffic. Turning right, which would take him to Paula's flat, always required a long wait at this time of day. Turning left, which would bring him to Jasmine, was much easier, and as soon as there was a gap in the traffic he did this, barely conscious of having made the decision.

The shabby door was opened immediately: they must have seen him coming down the area steps. Jasmine, looking much younger now that she was unsuspicious and happier, almost leapt at him.

'We've heard from Emma!'

Jasmine's mother, tall, thin, and tired-looking, welcomed him more calmly.

'I'm so glad you've come back. We were

174

wondering how to get hold of you. Emma telephoned just five minutes ago. She's with her father. They are staying somewhere in the South of England for a week or two. She didn't say where, but she sounded quite calm and not at all afraid.'

As she spoke, they had been walking towards the living-room. Books and papers lying on the big table had been pushed to one end, and on the other end there was a striped red and white tablecloth on which tea was set out.

A chair was placed for James, and after a brief hesitation he sat down, knowing that he was going to be late for Margaret's dinner, but in a childish way rather enjoying this gesture of defiance.

Besides, he had had nothing to eat all day and the plate full of bread and butter, with home-made raspberry jam alongside, was irresistible.

'I wonder where Emma is,' he said, helping himself generously to the raspberry jam and thinking, even as he was speaking, that if the child had been in touch with her friends, surely she would have made other calls as well.

'If she phones again,' said Jasmine's mother, 'shall I ask her to call you too?'

'Yes please, Mrs.—?'

'My name is Betty.'

'And mine is James. I'm actually on the

way to Emma's aunt at the moment. Paula is there. You know about Paula, don't you?'

'Emma told me,' said Jasmine after a glance at her mother. 'She said she and Paula had had an interesting talk about books. She also said—'

Jasmine broke off and again looked at her mother.

'Go on,' said Betty. 'James won't mind.'

'Emma said that her father was very impressed by Paula,' continued Jasmine. 'He thought she was clever and strong-minded and that's the sort of woman he likes.'

James listened to the child's remarks with the slight sense of shock that he always experienced when any other man showed an interest in Paula. It wasn't jealousy, he assured himself; it was more like the sort of surprise you feel when somebody admires a piece of your furniture that is so familiar to you that you no longer notice it.

'Perhaps she reminded him of Emma's mother,' he said thoughtfully, looking first at Jasmine and then at Betty. 'Did you know her well?' he added.

'We knew her, of course, as a neighbour,' replied Betty, 'but actually she was away rather a lot.'

'I told him,' interrupted Jasmine, speaking with her mouth full, which drew a mild rebuke from her mother. 'He wanted to know if she was on drugs,' added the child after hastily swallowing the mouthful.

'Did you?' asked Betty, turning to James and frowning slightly.

'Look, this isn't just idle curiosity,' said James. 'It was something I overheard, and I'm pursuing it because I thought it might help to find out why Paula has been so badly treated at the Windsor Clinic. There's been something going on there that the authorities want to hush up. Paula stumbled on it by chance, and they are afraid she will give them away. Actually she doesn't know anything specific—it's just vague suspicions, but neither of us is going to rest until we get to the bottom of it. And whatever it is, it's somehow tied up with Emma's folks. Has Emma talked to you about it?'

Mother and daughter glanced at each other. 'Emma believes her father has behaved very foolishly and got mixed up in some shady accounting business,' replied Betty at last. 'She doesn't say what she thinks it is, but she says she is determined to protect him if she can. That's why she's gone away with him. There was no need for her to go. She could have stayed with us.'

'And her mother's death?' prompted James.

'She won't talk about it, not even to Jasmine.'

'Do you know anything about it?' asked James. 'I gather it was some sort of drug overdose,' he added, as Betty seemed disinclined to reply.

'Yes,' said Betty, and then she turned to Jasmine and said, 'You're going to miss your telly programme if you don't hurry. Take the cake with you.'

'Oh gosh!' exclaimed the child, and ran out of the room.

'She's doing a project on conserving natural resources,' explained her mother. 'Fortunately there's something about it showing now, since I'd rather not talk about Linda Fielding's death in front of her.'

James sympathised. 'Did she die at home?'

'Linda took the drugs at home—a mix of sleeping pills and tranquillisers—but she actually died at the clinic, where she was taken as an emergency.'

'The Windsor Clinic?'

'Yes.'

'Who by?'

'Her husband, of course. Who else?'

'Tony Fielding, Emma's father.' And Margaret's brother, James added to himself, who arranged for Margaret to be transferred from the hospital casualty department to the Windsor Clinic after her accident. But Linda Fielding had been taken straight there, which was perhaps understandable since it was very near to her home and her husband had personal contacts there.

'So she actually died in the clinic,' said

178

James.

'Yes,' replied Betty shortly.

'Was her sister-in-law, Mrs. Leeming, with her?'

'I believe so. She'd come to stay with Mr. Fielding to look after Emma when her mother was away ill. If you think there's something not quite right about the way Emma's mother's death was dealt with,' added Betty with determination, 'then I've got to admit that I have had my suspicions too, but I don't want to talk about it or pursue it any further. For Emma's sake, for everybody's sake, it's much better left alone.'

'I'm sorry.' James sounded very contrite. 'I ought not to be bothering you like this. I'll direct my questions to another quarter.'

'You'd much better leave it alone altogether.'

'I'm sure you're right, but it isn't for my sake, it's for somebody else who's very close to me and who needs to know.'

Betty suddenly smiled. The tired face showed signs of humour and charm. 'Have some more cake,' she said.

'I'd love to, but I really do have to go now. If you hear any more from Emma, I'd be awfully grateful if you'd let me know, and I'd like to have a phone call from her if possible.'

'Where will you be?'

James paused before coming to a decision. 'I'll be at home. Here's my card. Not tonight, but from tomorrow. And thank you very much for all your kindness and hospitality. I hope all goes well with Jasmine's preservation project.'

They parted with goodwill. At least he had not bungled this interview, thought James as he drove away. It had given him and Paula plenty to think about, when they had a chance to talk in private. And it had made up his mind for him. From tomorrow he would be back at home. Tonight could not be avoided, but that would be the last time he stayed under the Leemings' roof.

Tomorrow he would take Paula away, and himself as well. Paula could go to the place Louise had suggested. She would soon recover and they would revert to their normal lives. A short holiday before the next university term began. Somewhere peaceful. One of the little Welsh seaside towns, perhaps.

This train of thought lasted him until he reached Paula's attic flat. The big room was unnaturally tidy, not a single book on the floor, nor a trail of cigarette ash to be seen. It occurred to him then that Paula had not been smoking at all since the operation. Perhaps she'll be able to kick the habit at last, he said to himself, but the prospect did not give entire satisfaction. He was so used to Paula smoking and to his own nagging her about it that it would feel almost like a loss were she to stop.

Now don't get sentimental, he scolded himself as he glanced through her letters, discarding the junk mail, and don't waste time. He would stop on the way, he decided, and phone Margaret to say that he had been held up by the traffic. And then he would have to remember not to say anything about what he had been doing when the inevitable questions came. She wouldn't believe him, of course. She would know perfectly well what he had been up to. In fact it would be much better to come straight out with it, be completely honest, and thus avoid the sort of verbal fencing that was an essential element in the attraction that Margaret held for him.

That would get them through the meal, and then he would insist on having a long talk with Paula alone, taking no notice of Margaret's protests that Paula wasn't fit for it. And as soon as the household had gone to bed, James would return to Paula's room and not leave it again without Paula.

Tomorrow morning he would bring her back to London. If it could be done openly, with gratitude to the Leemings and no sign of suspicion or ill will, so much the better. But if not, then there would have to be yet another 'abduction.' James had no doubt that he could achieve this. He certainly seemed to be getting enough practice in the art.

CHAPTER FIFTEEN

Paula propped herself up against the pillows and switched on the radio. One of those political discussions was taking place where the interviewer was attempting to get the speaker to admit what they both knew perfectly well that he was never going to admit—a ritual that could be soothing or irritating, according to one's own state of mind.

At the moment Paula found it comfortingly remote from reality. The talk with Margaret had disturbed her, and she could not easily recapture the sense of dreamy well-being that she had experienced earlier. During a slight pause in the flow of words she could hear footsteps on the stairs, and a moment later there was a knock at the door.

It didn't sound like Margaret's knock, and the thought that it could be James brought a momentary lift of the heart.

'Come in!' called Paula, switching off the radio and easing herself up to sit on the edge of the bed.

The head of Professor Guy Leeming appeared round the door. 'Am I disturbing you? I hope you weren't asleep.'

'Not at all. Do come in.'

Paula was almost as glad to see him as she would have been to see James.

'Margaret's down the garden picking vegetables,' said Guy, moving over to the chair. 'She's a great gardener. I'm afraid I'm useless in that respect—as in so many other matters of daily life.'

'One can't do everything,' said Paula consolingly.

'Are you a gardener?'

'Not in a top-floor flat in London. But I was brought up by my grandparents, who kept a market garden, and I once used to know something about it.'

'That's interesting,' said Guy, sounding as if he really meant it. 'Somehow one doesn't expect university lecturers—'

'I know,' said Paula. 'We have such preconceived ideas about people, don't we.'

'I suppose so,' said Guy vaguely and then remained silent, looking, thought Paula, rather old and tired and depressed. But I don't feel in the mood to try to cheer him up, she added to herself; after all, I'm the one who's the invalid.

After a long pause he seemed to recollect this himself, and enquired whether she was comfortable and had everything she needed. Paula assured him that she was very comfortable, and repeated her thanks for their kindness and her apologies for being such a trouble to them.

183

'You're no trouble to me,' said Guy, 'and Margaret loves to have somebody to fuss over.'

Paula could find nothing to say to this. She was beginning to think that he ought to go away now, having carried out his social duties, when he suddenly said, in quite a different tone of voice, 'Have you known James Goff for long?'

'Yes,' replied Paula, doing a hasty calculation. 'About fifteen years, I suppose.'

'What's he like as a scholar?'

'He hasn't published much,' replied Paula, 'but he's a very good teacher.'

What Guy really wants to know, she was saying to herself as she spoke, is whether James is any threat to his marriage. So he does notice things after all; he isn't completely wrapped up in his own affairs, and if I go very carefully and don't say the wrong thing, I might learn something more about Margaret.

'I suppose it is rather discouraging to one's own efforts,' said Guy, 'being descended from a genius like G. E. Goff.'

'Luckily James hasn't got any literary ambitions,' said Paula. 'He knows his own limitations.'

'You know him well?' It was as much a statement as a question.

'Very well,' replied Paula. 'In fact—' She hesitated and then took the plunge. 'In fact

184

we're thinking of getting married sometime before long.'

Guy didn't look surprised, but neither did he look as reassured as she had expected. He murmured something about wishing them well and then sunk into silence.

Paula decided that it was her turn now.

'Have you and Margaret been married for long?'

'Less than a year.'

'I love your house.'

'Do you? It was Margaret's choice, but I'm rather fond of it too. My wife—I mean my former wife—and I had been talking of moving out of London at the time of her death.'

Paula made encouraging noises; this looked like being interesting.

'We had actually decided on Sussex and were looking at houses when Alice's condition suddenly worsened, as it sometimes does with cancer. She had a morbid dread of hospitals and so we had agency nurses in to look after her at home. Margaret was one of them. She cared for Alice most devotedly.'

'Then your first wife was never in a nursing-home?'

'Never. She never left home.'

'I just wondered whether she had been in the Windsor Clinic,' explained Paula. 'I believe Margaret did some nursing there.'

'Among other places. Margaret worked for years as an agency nurse. She preferred it to a permanent job.'

'Had she been married before?'

'Er, yes. It didn't last long.'

'Neither did mine,' said Paula, wondering at Guy's air of embarrassment. He obviously missed his Alice badly, and no doubt for this reason felt drawn towards Alice's nurse, but it rather looked as if he didn't trust Margaret and was afraid of being made a fool of. Did he know about Jack? Probably not. Which would give Jack a hold over Margaret. But if Jack had this hold over her, why did he have to go to such extremes to stop her talking?

There are some missing pieces here, decided Paula, something I just don't know about, and maybe Guy doesn't know either. But he's filled in a bit more of the picture; maybe James can put in yet more pieces.

'Margaret is a very fascinating person,' she said aloud. 'I felt that the moment I met her in the Windsor Clinic, when she told me she was married to you. I also got the impression that she was devoted to her home.'

Even as she was speaking, Paula felt that she was being both intrusive and condescending, but her remarks seemed to please Guy. It looks as if he really cares for her, thought Paula, not just as a housekeeper, and he's capable of being painfully jealous.

186

'Was Margaret actually living with her brother and sister-in-law?' she asked.

'Oh no,' was Guy's reply. 'She spent a lot of time there—her brother's wife was a bit of an invalid, and Margaret was always very concerned for the child, but she did have a flat of her own not very far away.'

'In Hampstead?'

'Yes.' Guy stood up. 'I must go. Margaret is roasting a leg of lamb and I always make the mint sauce. That's the extent of my help in the house.' He smiled and gave the faintest sign of a wink. 'Actually I can cook quite well, but I don't mind not being allowed to.'

'I shall look forward to the mint sauce,' said Paula, smiling too.

After Guy had gone, she leant back and thought over their conversation. A picture of Guy's Margaret emerged from it which tallied with her own first impressions and with James's view of Margaret too. A woman capable of loyalty and devotion in her profession, yet at the same time unpredictable, perhaps even slightly unbalanced, but never boring.

A good actress, a most accomplished liar. 'Pretending,' her niece Emma had called it, and said that her own mother was the same. A germ of an idea began to stir in Paula's consciousness, but it was so faint and slippery that, like an unremembered name, she could not grasp it.

After a while she dozed a little. The idea seemed to have been emerging more clearly during her half-sleep, but her waking awareness could not quite deal with it. Filling her thoughts was the longing to see James, and the fact that she was hungry.

She looked at her watch. It was half past eight. Surely they should be eating dinner now. 'I'm going down to see what's happening,' said Paula aloud.

The walking was still an effort, and she was glad to cling to the stair-rail.

Guy met her in the hall. He was looking very anxious. 'Come and sit in the living-room,' he said, taking her arm. 'I didn't want to disturb you, but I'm so glad you've come. I don't know what's happened to Margaret. I can't find her anywhere in the garden or in the house. James phoned about half an hour ago. He's been held up by the traffic, but he ought to be here any time now.'

Paula, feeling a little giddy, sat down to digest this news. 'What are you going to do?' she asked after a few moments' silence.

Guy produced a faint smile. 'I've turned off the oven so that the meat doesn't burn and I'm going to get us some tea and biscuits now, and as soon as James comes we'll take some vegetables from the freezer and have a meal.'

188

He disappeared into the kitchen and came back a few minutes later with the tea. Paula ate and drank gratefully.

'Have you any idea where she might have gone?' she asked. 'Has Margaret done this sort of thing before?'

'Not exactly,' was the answer, 'but she is a little—shall we say impulsive—at times. No, I've no idea where she is. Unless it's something to do with Emma.'

'She told me Emma had rung earlier this evening. Could they have arranged to meet?'

Guy agreed that it was possible.

'But why didn't she tell you?' asked Paula. He merely shrugged in reply.

Paula took a biscuit and sat thinking while she ate. Perhaps Tony was in serious trouble; perhaps Guy knew more than he was saying; perhaps it would be better not to make any more comments to him. When James came, he could take over.

And then a horrible thought struck her. Supposing James didn't come. Supposing he and Margaret had arranged this between them, to meet and run away together, leaving Guy and Paula to console each other!

The thought was so appalling that she could not stop herself from exclaiming aloud, 'Guy, do you think it's possible that James—'

He interrupted her, reading her mind. 'I've been thinking of that too, but I think it

189

depends very much on James. You know him well, I hardly know him. Would he do such a thing?'

Paula relaxed a little. 'No. No, I don't think so. No, I'm quite sure he's incapable of it. And in any case'—her words were now tumbling over each other in her attempt to reassure herself—'if he did have something like that in mind he would never have rung to say that he was on his way.'

'He wouldn't have called me,' said Guy, 'but he might have called Margaret.'

'Not at the time he did call. If they'd had an arrangement he'd have known she'd be gone by then.'

'That's true.' Guy brightened up a little. 'Anyway, we shall soon know. He'll either arrive or he'll ring again, and meanwhile I'm going to make us some sandwiches. I think we'll forget about the roast lamb. Does that suit you?'

'It does indeed. And I'll come and help.'

Guy protested, but Paula insisted that it would do her good to make herself useful, instead of being an invalid to be waited on, and promised she would sit down and not exert herself.

They both moved to the kitchen and set to work.

How odd, thought Paula, that in spite of the circumstances, I should feel rather contented, sitting here at the kitchen table

190

and cutting bread, with Professor Guy Leeming opposite me spreading butter very generously.

Bread and butter. There was something very ordinary and very comforting about it: it just didn't go with tragedy. Guy glanced up, saw her smiling to herself, and asked what the joke was.

'I was thinking of Thackeray's summing up of Goethe,' she said:

> "Charlotte, having seen his body
> Borne before her on a shutter,
> Like a well-conducted person
> Went on cutting bread and butter."

One just can't take *The Sorrows of Werther* too seriously after reading that.'

'No indeed,' said Guy. 'May I ask a rather personal question?'

'Go ahead.'

'Do you and James—I am taking it that you spend a good deal of time together—do you and James talk much about the teaching of English literature—and literature in general?'

'No, I don't think we do,' said Paula after a short pause. 'Certainly not as much as we used to. One doesn't, not when one has known somebody for a long time and been teaching something for many years. One gets rather tired of it.'

'Exactly,' said Guy as if he had scored a big debating point. 'Then you can imagine that I am glad to be married to a woman who has no more than the average educated person's interest in books.'

'I can,' said Paula. 'What do you and Margaret talk about?'

'Cooking, modern art, various domestic details, people we know, and—I'm rather ashamed to say—horror films. That is, we don't talk about them, we just watch them.'

'It sounds a good selection for domestic harmony,' said Paula lightly, and she had an almost overwhelming impulse to add, 'Guy—do you really love Margaret very much?' but managed to control herself, saying instead that she thought that was enough bread cut and what should she do now.

'Chop up some cheese and tomato,' said Guy.

Paula had only just started on this when there was a ring at the door. 'James!' she cried, and got to her feet too quickly, giving an involuntary little cry of pain. Guy begged her to take care, and she assured him that the last thing she wanted was to be back in a nursing-home again. The bell rang once more as she made her slow way to the front door, and she was very conscious that Guy had come to the kitchen door and was watching her.

Paula believed that this was because of Guy's concern for her, and not because of any curiosity to see how she and James greeted each other, but nevertheless it troubled her because she was herself so unsure about how she stood with James.

There was an inner door that was normally left open except at night, and she half closed this behind her before opening the main door.

The lamp in the porch was not yet switched on, but there was still light in the sky this late summer evening. Her first impression was that whoever it was had got tired of waiting and had gone away again. But she was expecting to see a tall adult. When she looked down instead of up she saw a child standing there, a girl of about twelve years old, staring at her with almost as much surprise as Paula herself was showing.

'Emma!' cried Paula. 'How on earth did you get here?'

CHAPTER SIXTEEN

'Are you all right? Where's Auntie Margaret?' asked Emma.

'She's not here at the moment,' replied Paula, moving aside to let Emma pass. 'We're in the kitchen,' she added, and then suddenly she was overcome by weakness. 'I've got to sit down,' she muttered, and stumbled over to the living-room.

She felt for a chair, sank into it, shut her eyes, and heard voices as if from a distance.

'Is she all right, Uncle Guy? She looks very pale.'

'Run into the kitchen and pour a cup of tea. And put plenty of sugar into it.'

Five minutes later Paula was recovering from her giddy attack and bemoaning her feeble state.

'You ought to be in bed,' said Emma in a severe and very adult manner. 'Why isn't Auntie Margaret looking after you?'

Guy explained briefly. 'Have you any idea where she might have gone?' he asked in conclusion.

'Perhaps she's gone to meet Dad,' replied Emma after a moment's thought.

Guy and Paula looked at each other. 'We never thought of that,' said Paula.

'You wouldn't have known he was near here,' said Emma. 'We've been staying at Heath House, near Lark Heath. Dad's friendly with the matron there.' Emma's tone made it clear that this friendliness was not shared by herself.

'Now just a minute,' said Guy. 'Let's get this straight, Emma. Your father brought you here on his way to—do you know where he has gone?'

The child shook her head. 'He wouldn't tell me. He said it was very important and he'd call here for me late this evening or tomorrow morning.'

'And who did he expect to look after you?'

'Auntie Margaret, of course.'

'Suppose she hadn't been here—in fact she isn't here. Suppose there had been nobody here.'

Guy was beginning to sound disapproving, and Emma to sound indignant.

Paula intervened. 'Well, there's one thing clear—if Emma's father expected Margaret to be here, then he can't have arranged to meet her elsewhere.' She glanced at Emma enquiringly.

Emma bit her lip and looked away. 'It was silly of me to suggest it,' she muttered.

'You're tired,' said Paula. 'And hungry too, I expect. So are we. Why don't we eat those sandwiches?'

Guy took the hint and got up to go to the kitchen. The other two sat in silence for a little while, and then Emma said in a low voice, 'Paula, I want to tell you something.'

'I'm listening.'

'Dad didn't bring me here. He thinks I'm still at Heath House with the matron. But I can't stand her and I hate it there. It's all rich people who have gone a bit mad—at least they're supposed to be and I'm not supposed to talk to the patients, but I don't think some

195

of them are mad at all but anyway that's not what I want to tell you. It's about Dad. I'm frightened. I'm sure he's gone to do something silly. Or maybe he's run away somewhere else where he can't take me with him.'

'What makes you think that?' asked Paula.

'He had a phone call that I didn't manage to listen to, as I usually do. Then he went to talk to the matron and I couldn't hear that either. And then he came back to me and said he'd got to go out urgently and he might not be back until tomorrow morning and I was to stay with the matron, and I tried to find out what it was about and to get him to take me too, but he wouldn't. And after he'd gone I got more and more scared and I decided to come here. There's a man who visits one of the patients whom I talk to sometimes, and he lives quite near here, and he brought me to the gate.'

'And if we'd all been out—'

'I'd have gone to this man and asked him to take me to London,' was the defiant reply.

'Emma,' said Paula very earnestly, 'do you know why your father is running away?'

'Because of the drug money, of course,' replied the child, opening her eyes wide in surprise at the question. 'There's an enquiry going on into Dad's business, particularly Mr. Easebourne's accounts, and he's afraid they might bring in the police. But he said yesterday that he thought they were going to get away with it and that Chris had done a very good job.'

'Chris?'

'Christopher Peach.' Emma made a face. 'The guy whose car ran into me and Auntie Margaret. He works for Dad. Dad thinks he's marvellous. I think he's yukky.'

'Slick accountant?' said Paula.

'Slimy,' said Emma vigorously.

Paula looked keenly at the child, who was perched on the arm of one of the chairs, swinging a blue-trousered leg backwards and forwards. She was going to be tall, like her father, and had the same longish face and slightly prominent nose, but the eyes and mouth were very different. They showed both intelligence and determination.

Like her mother? From what Paula had heard of Linda Fielding it did not appear that she had been a particularly strong character, not like her sister-in-law Margaret, for instance. And yet Linda's young daughter appeared to feel that she must take on her mother's job of looking after Tony.

There was something rather puzzling here which suddenly, in Paula's mind, tied up with the elusive ideas that had been tantalising her earlier. Impulsively she said, 'Emma, did your mother ever—' She broke off when Guy came into the room carrying a

197

tray, but in any case, at the mention of her mother, Emma's face had taken on a closed look.

Paula subsided. She was not sorry to relax and put aside her speculations while she ate. It seemed that anxiety had not dulled the appetite, because the other two also ate eagerly and said very little.

When the plates were empty, Guy said to Emma, 'If your father has gone to London, he'll be there by now. I'm going to phone your flat.'

Emma protested that she could do it herself, but Guy waved her aside. 'There's probably some perfectly simple explanation,' he said, 'and we must try not to get too imaginative.'

He picked up the telephone, obtained the number, and waited. At last he said, 'Who's there? Who is that? I'm trying to contact Mr. Fielding.'

Paula and Emma, watching anxiously, saw his face contract in annoyance before he replaced the phone.

'What happened?' asked Paula.

'Somebody picked it up and said nothing and continued to say nothing and then cut off.'

Emma was becoming very agitated. 'Uncle, Uncle Guy, I think we ought to go and see what's happened to Dad. It might be the police there. Supposing somebody promised him it was safe and he could come home, but it wasn't safe and the police have caught up with him. Please, Uncle Guy, let's go, let's go!'

Guy looked disconcerted by this onslaught. His attempts at sympathetic reassurance were not very successful and at last he said, rather abruptly, 'We can't possibly go rushing up to London now, Emma, and leave Paula alone. Could you please pass me that telephone directory?'

Emma obeyed, asking what he was going to do.

'Contact the police and ask them to investigate.'

'No, no!' Emma flung herself at him again. 'Not the police! Suppose Dad really is there!'

'Now listen, Emma, my dear,' said Guy. 'I know it's very difficult for you, but you know that your Auntie Margaret and I love you very much and will always look after you. If your father has broken the law, then sooner or later he is going to be found out and you will have to face it.'

'No, no.' The child ran to Paula. 'Stop him, stop him!'

Paula was more successful than Guy in bringing comfort. Over Emma's head, she looked at him and said, 'Isn't there some other way we can find out? If we wait till James comes, and he must surely be here soon—'

'I've got it!' Emma raised her head from Paula's shoulder. 'We'll ask Jasmine and her mum to go and look. They're in the flat—downstairs.'

This suggestion was welcomed with relief by both Paula and Guy. Emma, recovering herself with surprising speed, made the call. She listened for a while and then turned to the others.

'Jasmine's mum has gone to look. They've been watching "Crime Busters" on telly and didn't hear anything upstairs through all that noise. They don't have a key, but they'll be able to see if any lights are on.'

'And whether your father's car is parked nearby,' said Guy.

'Jasmine's doing that now. Here she is.' Emma listened again, then told the others. 'Dad's car is parked opposite. All the others parked near are the usual ones, except there's a little red car and a big white one further up the road. And some others that Jasmine doesn't know. She thinks they're to do with the pop group house. Here's her mum coming back. Would you like to speak to her, Uncle Guy?'

'Thank you, Emma.' Guy took the phone, introduced himself, and said, 'Could you wait a moment? Emma's going to listen on the other line.' He signalled to Emma. 'In the study— the phone's on the desk.'

Emma ran off.

'There isn't much to tell,' said Jasmine's mother at the other end of the line. 'There's light showing in the hall and between the curtains upstairs. I rang the bell by the entry-phone and Mr. Fielding answered. He said, "Who's that?" and I said who I was and he asked if it was very urgent because he'd got someone with him and they were having a very important talk.'

'How did Dad sound?' broke in Emma.

'Just as usual. Maybe a bit impatient,' was the reply. 'It's difficult to tell on the entry-phone.'

'So what did you say?' asked Guy.

'I said I'd had a call from Emma and she was very worried about him, and he said to tell Emma that he was fine and he'd either be with her or call her first thing in the morning.'

From the study line came a little exclamation from Emma. On the line in the living-room Guy asked, 'And that was all?'

'Yes,' replied Jasmine's mother.

'And you got the impression that he wasn't alone?'

'Definitely. He sounded like somebody who'd been interrupted.'

'Not alarmed, worried, or anything like that?'

'No, just rather impatient.'

'It sounds like Dad when he's busy,' said Emma wistfully, adding in a low voice,

'Didn't he tell you to send me his love?'

'Of course he did, just before he rang off,' said Jasmine's mother rather quickly.

'Hold on a minute,' said Guy. 'There's our front doorbell. Emma, are you still there? Would you go and answer it?'

'Okay.'

There was a click on the line as Emma put down the phone.

'You wanted to tell me something,' said Guy, 'without Emma hearing. Am I right?'

'Yes, thank you, Professor Leeming. But I didn't want to alarm or distress Emma. Actually her father didn't sound at all at ease. He sounded hurried and worried, and he certainly didn't remember to send her his love.'

'Do you know him well?'

'Yes, quite well. As a neighbour. Not as a personal friend.'

'So you wouldn't mistake his voice—it couldn't have been somebody else speaking?'

'I did wonder for a moment. These entry-phones do distort the voice badly, but I've no reason to suppose it wasn't Mr. Fielding.'

'Thank you very much. I'd better go now. There's someone coming. But I'll be in touch.'

'And I'll call you if anything happens.'

Guy put down the phone and went out into the hall. James, looking rather

202

bewildered, was coming towards him. Emma was clinging with both hands to James's arm.

'Ah, at last,' said Guy with heartfelt relief.

'I'm awfully sorry I'm so late,' said James. 'There was an accident just at the end of the motorway and a big hold-up. Where is Margaret? How is Paula?'

'Paula's in the living-room,' said Guy, walking back towards the door. The others followed him in a rush, and then they all stopped short just inside the door. Paula was lying right back in the big armchair. She was breathing slowly and evenly and there was a peaceful expression on her face. When they all moved forward she didn't stir, but when Emma ran up to her and cried anxiously, 'Are you all right?' she opened her eyes and smiled faintly, then muttered, 'Very tired,' before going to sleep again.

'Margaret would be very angry with me,' said Guy to James when the latter returned from getting Paula to bed. 'To tell the truth I was so concerned with trying to track down Emma's father that I forgot about Paula. She's not meant to be sitting up so long, and she's certainly not meant to have all this excitement. Do you think we ought to send for the doctor?'

James thought not. 'Rest and peace of mind, that's all she needs. I'm taking her back to London tomorrow. One of the Windsor Clinic nurses has recommended a convalescent home. Where is Emma?'

'Making you some sandwiches,' replied Guy. 'I'm trying to get her to go to bed too, but she says she can't rest until she knows for sure that her father is all right. I'd better tell you—' and Guy briefly related the gist of the phone call to Emma's friends. James countered with a summary of his afternoon's activities. 'So what's become of Margaret?' he concluded abruptly.

'Paula and I thought she might possibly be with you,' said Guy, and then hurried on, 'but it sounds as if she heard there was danger to her brother and has gone to try to avert it.'

'Then why didn't she tell you?' asked James.

'Because she knows what I think of him, I suppose,' was Guy's reply.

They looked at each other, exchanging thoughts without uttering them.

'After all, he is Emma's father,' said Guy at last.

'If he were here, under your roof,' said James, 'would you try to save him from being arrested?'

'No,' was the prompt reply. 'Would you?'

'No.'

Again they looked at each other. 'I'm not going to leave Paula tonight,' added James.

'Emma still wants me to take her to London,' muttered Guy. 'I suppose I'll have to go.'

James looked at his watch. 'Half past ten. There's a train at eleven from Gatwick. You could be in Hampstead by midnight if you go at once.'

'I can't drive,' said Guy, standing up, 'and in any case Margaret's taken the car. But the garage in the village can usually supply a taxi at short notice. I suppose you wouldn't drive us down there to save time?'

'Yes, I'll do that,' replied James after a moment's thought. 'Paula's asleep. She'll be all right for ten minutes or so.'

CHAPTER SEVENTEEN

Paula was having a dream. It was not a particularly alarming dream. In fact she was in what had become a very familiar situation during the past week. She was lying in bed—she did not know where, but it did not matter much because she knew she was being looked after. In fact it was quite pleasant just to lie there and know that she needn't bother about anything at all.

She was thirsty, and somebody—she didn't know who— brought her some orange juice. Then she was too hot, and somebody rearranged the bedclothes. And then somebody said it was time for her next injection, and it all felt quite natural and normal and nothing mattered at all. And so the dream flowed on.

★   ★   ★

James returned to the Leemings' house to find the driveway blocked by a car that was turning round to reverse into the garage. He waited, looking up at the house. Had he really left so many lights burning?

The car in front moved into the garage and its lights were turned off. James drove quickly up to the front door, hurriedly got out of his car, and using Guy's keys, let himself into the house and ran upstairs. It would have been natural, in normal circumstances, to wait for Margaret to come out of the garage so that they could enter her house together, but at the moment he had thoughts for nothing but Paula.

He had left the bedside lamp burning; it would have been comforting for her if she woke while he was away. She stirred when he came into the room, opened her eyes, and smiled faintly.

'Hullo, James.'

'Feeling better, darling?'

'I'm sorry to be so useless. What's going on?'

'Guy has taken Emma to London. She's afraid the police may have caught up with her father. Margaret's just got back. I'll go and talk to her in a moment. Tomorrow morning you are going to a convalescent home in Hampstead recommended by your nurse friend Louise, and there you are going to stay until you are completely recovered.'

'James, I've been thinking—'

'So have I. Listen, love, I must go and see Margaret. I'll be back as soon as I can and we'll talk. As much as you feel fit for.'

'Don't be too long,' said Paula. 'And could you pass me the orange juice?'

James looked around, found the glass of water, and passed it to her. 'Sorry, love, can't see any juice,' he said.

'But I thought—oh, it must have been a dream. A funny dream,' murmured Paula as she drank. 'See you later.'

'Back soon.'

James left the door slightly ajar, and looked along the passage to the top of the stairs. He had half expected to see Margaret coming up towards him, but there was no sound nor sign of her. He found her at last in the kitchen, contemplating an overcooked and congealing joint of lamb as if it was her only care in the world.

'Sorry about this,' she said in a most matter-of-fact voice. 'I'll make it up into something for dinner tomorrow.'

'I shan't be here for dinner tomorrow,' said James in similar tones. 'And nor will

Paula. I'm taking her to a convalescent home in London. We can't impose on you and Guy any longer, but we are most grateful for your help in an emergency.'

She made no reply, but looked straight at him, smiling slightly. Or was it a sneer and not a smile? Mystery woman, Mona Lisa, thought James.

She spoke at last. 'Has Guy gone to bed?'

'No. He's gone to London.'

'To London?' She frowned. 'Why?'

'To find out what's happened to Emma's father. Emma turned up here very worried about him. But I suppose you know all about that.'

'You suppose wrongly. I was called away suddenly on very urgent business, and I got home as soon as I could. I should be grateful for any information you can give me about my husband, my brother, and my niece. It so happens that I am rather concerned for their welfare. All of them.'

'Emma has been at Heath House with her father,' replied James very calmly. 'He went away this afternoon, Emma believes in connection with the money-laundering activities. She made her way here, hoping to find you, but found only Guy and Paula. As soon as I got here, Guy felt he could leave Paula, and Emma persuaded him to take her to London, home to Tony's flat.'

'When did they go?'

208

Margaret sounded genuinely anxious, but James, determined not to trust any action, any word of hers, answered coolly.

'Not long before you arrived. They were getting a train and then a taxi.'

'Oh, my God.'

She put a hand to her forehead. It was a beautifully controlled theatrical gesture. James regarded it dispassionately.

'If I go at once,' she went on as if to herself, 'I might just get there first. I've got to be with Emma.'

As she spoke, she put on the jacket that she had just taken off, picked up her handbag, took the car keys. James was puzzled. This wasn't acting. Surely here was genuine fear and apprehension. He fought back the desire to sympathise, to ask questions, and remained silent, waiting to see what she would do next.

Without saying another word, without even looking in his direction, Margaret hurried out of the room, across the hall, and out of the house. James followed, feeling more and more puzzled, even slightly alarmed. By the light in the porch he watched her go to the garage and open the door. Then came the sound of an engine about to fire, but it suddenly spluttered and stopped.

Silence followed. Battery? James asked himself; or something more serious? What would she do next? She was out of her car and coming towards him even as he mentally asked the question.

'James.' The voice was a mixture of command and appeal. 'It's imperative that I get to London as soon as possible. May I borrow your car? I promise to take care of it.'

'I'm sorry,' he replied. 'It's only insured for myself. Would you like me to have a look at yours? Or shall we call the AA?'

'There isn't time. I've got to go at once.'

She really was desperate; he was convinced of that now.

'I'd drive you myself,' he said, 'if there was someone trustworthy here to look after Paula.'

'Thanks. We can soon fix that up.'

She was back in the house immediately, at the phone in the living-room, calling a number. There followed a brief conversation.

'Dr. Wimborne's wife is coming herself,' said Margaret as she replaced the phone. 'She's an experienced nurse and a very calm and comfortable person. Paula couldn't be in better hands. She'll be here in fifteen minutes. What speed will your Renault do?'

James did not reply. He was eating the sandwiches that Emma had made for him earlier. The silence persisted as he poured coffee into a cup, sipped at it, made a face, and replaced the cup. Margaret left the room

210

and returned within a couple of minutes with a steaming mug of instant coffee.

'Thanks,' said James. 'What about you?'

He looked up at her. She shook her head. All the vitality seemed to have gone out of her and she looked tired, worried, and old. It was at that moment that he decided he really would drive her to London, provided that he approved of the doctor's wife and that Paula agreed to his going.

'Excuse me,' he muttered and left the room.

Upstairs, Paula still lay peacefully in bed, eyes closed and breathing slow and steady. James leant over her.

'Darling—I'm sorry to disturb you. It's only for a minute. Are you listening?'

'M'm. Yes.' Paula's hand moved over the bedcover, feeling for his. Her eyes remained closed.

'I've got to leave you for a while,' said James. 'The doctor's wife, who is a nurse, is coming to be with you. Will that be all right?'

'Yes,' said Paula more clearly, opening her eyes for a moment and shutting them again. 'I'm fine—just terribly sleepy. Where's Margaret?'

'Gone to London. There's some new crisis arisen over her brother.'

'And Emma?'

'Gone to London with Guy. I want to follow and see what's going on. Mrs.

211

Wimborne will be here in a moment and will stay till I get back. If you could just try to keep awake till she comes.'

Paula's fingers pressed his hand and her lips moved in a smile. 'Have you discovered something?'

'I'm hoping to,' he replied.

'Sorry I'm so dopey. I'd love to talk. I've been thinking...'

'Yes, love?'

'Tony's wife, Emma's mother. I've been wondering whether...'

James bent closer to listen. 'So have I been wondering,' he said. 'Try and wake up a little and tell me more.'

Paula, obviously with a great effort, raised herself on one elbow and took a deep breath. At that very moment came a knock on the door and a slight fair middle-aged woman came into the room and introduced herself to James. Then she walked over to the bed and laid a hand first on Paula's forehead and then on her wrist. 'Mrs. Glenning,' she said, 'I'm Mrs. Wimborne. I'll be sitting here reading until the others come home. If you want anything, just tell me.'

'I only want to sleep,' said Paula.

'That's fine.' Mrs. Wimborne turned to James. 'There's no need to worry about her, truly, Mr. Goff. What she needs is a good night's sleep, and if you'll excuse my saying so, you look as if you could do with one too.'

James smiled wanly. 'I certainly could, but I'll survive. After all, I'm not recovering from an operation.'

They moved towards the door. 'Mrs. Wimborne,' he said, holding it open and standing in the corridor just outside, 'it's extremely kind of you to come at short notice like this.'

'Oh, I don't mind at all. I'm very pleased to be able to help Professor and Mrs. Leeming.'

'Have you known them for long?'

'Professor Leeming for many years, and Mrs. Leeming since she was nursing Professor Leeming's first wife. Goodbye, Mr. Goff. It's very kind of you to help Margaret in this new trouble about her wretched brother.'

'Goodbye. Thanks again.'

Feeling considerably reassured, James hurried downstairs. To see Margaret through other eyes, to see Margaret himself as tired and anxious, careless of what impression she was giving, was producing in him a more balanced attitude towards her. I'm going to make it quite clear to her, he told himself, that there's going to be no relationship between us. And I'm going to ask her some straight questions; if she answers, well and good, and if not, then I'll have to find the answers some other way.

For the first few minutes of the drive

neither of them spoke. Then Margaret broke the silence.

'James—I'm enormously grateful to you.'

'That's all right. Now I know that Paula's being looked after, I'm actually quite interested to be in at the kill.'

'At the kill? What do you mean?' she asked sharply.

'Nothing in particular. You tell me. You're the one who knows what's going on. You're so desperate to get to Tony's flat that you must be afraid of something pretty drastic.'

'I'm afraid,' began Margaret, and paused for some time before going on. 'I'm afraid Tony may have done something silly.'

'Like killing someone? Like killing himself? Like letting somebody else kill him?'

'That I don't know.'

'I think you do know. I think you know exactly what you are afraid of. You may even have set the scene yourself.'

'I haven't!' cried Margaret, and James laughed triumphantly.

'What a simple trap to fall into! You of all people. Come on now, Margaret. Tell me all about it. It's Emma you're worried for. Genuinely worried. I don't believe you really care about anything in the world except Emma. And it's not that you're afraid of Emma finding out that her father has been

214

dabbling in the drugs trade, because she knows all about it already. You must be scared that she's going to find a fake suicide. Just like with her mother, Tony's wife Linda.'

'Linda didn't kill herself. It was an accident.'

'An overdose? An emergency at the Windsor Clinic? They don't have accidental overdoses at the Windsor. You know that from your own experiences. Someone tried to dope you into amnesia. Why? Because you knew how Linda died and you couldn't be relied on to keep quiet any longer. Linda died of an overdose, a deliberately contrived overdose. And was deliberately not revived, although her life could easily have been saved. Why did Tony want his wife to die?'

'Tony didn't want his wife to die!' cried Margaret, and then, on an even higher note, 'James!'

They had missed an oncoming car by inches as James did a dangerous piece of overtaking.

'Then who did want Linda dead?' James slowed down a little. 'Jack? Mrs. Kennedy? You yourself? Surely not Guy.'

Margaret made no reply.

'It's no good pretending you don't know, because you obviously know it all,' went on James. 'According to what Paula overheard, it definitely seems as if Jack was responsible

215

for overdosing you even if it was the matron who actually did the job. But why should Jack have killed Linda? Had she threatened to expose the drugs racket? Or had he—had he—'

James executed another risky manoeuvre, to the accompaniment of a stifled scream from Margaret. 'I've got it, I've got it now!' he shouted. 'Jack and Linda. Of course! It was Linda who was having an affair with Jack, not you. You were covering up for her. Linda was tired of her husband and craved for somebody more exciting. And Linda threatened Jack when the affair was over, or rather when she got too serious and he threw her over because he didn't want a messy divorce, he wanted a new rich wife. The glamorous Rachel maybe. She must be making a fortune out of that high-class loony-bin in Sussex.'

James slowed down and drove slowly along in the inner lane. Margaret remained silent. 'So who would want Linda dead,' he went on. 'Certainly Jack. He didn't want any bad publicity and he didn't want Tony to know. Tony was useful to him and very much under his influence, but when it came to Tony's own wife, the worm might turn. Perhaps Tony did find out and killed Linda in a fit of jealousy. Which would of course give Jack an even bigger hold over him.'

James paused before going on. 'Or maybe

somebody else was jealous too. Maybe Linda had supplanted you in Jack's very fluctuating affections. And maybe you were jealous of Linda already, because Linda had Emma, whom you truly love, and Linda had your brother, whom you both love and hate. Oh yes, there are several people who could have wished Linda dead.'

There was a short silence, and then Margaret said in a tired voice, 'Do you think we could postpone these extravagant speculations and go a bit faster now? But safely, please.'

'All right,' said James, speeding up. 'At least we agree on one thing—Emma must be spared as much as possible,' and for the rest of the way they barely spoke.

CHAPTER EIGHTEEN

James had difficulty in finding a parking place. Margaret wanted to get out and leave him to it, but he was determined that they should enter her brother's flat together. He stopped so near to a car parked opposite that Margaret could not open the passenger door. An argument was beginning to develop when luckily a car moved off and James manoeuvred hurriedly into the space.

'You've got the keys?' he asked as they

crossed the road.

'Of course.'

There was light showing between the curtains of the ground floor. There was also light in the basement. James caught Margaret's arm. 'Shouldn't we go first to Emma's friends? I'm sure that's where she'll be. If anything's happened to her father, then Guy will take her to her friends.'

'All right. You go downstairs. I'll go straight to Tony's.'

'No. We'll stick together.'

She knows, he was saying to himself. It's not only for Emma's sake that she's here. She knows what we are going to find and she wants to find it by herself. Why? To destroy some evidence? To protect somebody, or to protect herself? She's not to be trusted. Take care.

And for a moment James's mind flashed back to Paula, and he told himself very firmly that the doctor's wife was completely to be trusted; then they were at the front door of Tony's flat, and Margaret was pushing her way past him into the hall, then through the first door on the left. James looked over her shoulder, and nearly tripped when she stopped very suddenly just inside the room.

'Margaret! Where on earth have you been?' asked a familiar voice.

'Guy—oh, Guy!'

Margaret ran forward and clung to Guy, who was standing by the desk near to the big bay window. James followed more slowly, looking about him. They were in a large square comfortable room with high bookshelves and leather armchairs and a coal-effect fire. A man was sitting in one of the chairs by the fire. At first sight it looked as if he was asleep, with legs sprawled over the rug, arms lying loosely on the arms of the chair, and head leaning slightly to one side against a cushion.

James looked at Margaret, saw her move away from Guy and go to the man in the chair.

'Tony, Tony!'

Her back was turned towards James, so that he could not see the expression on her face as she spoke. Was she really expecting her brother to respond? Or had she known that this was what they would find?

She must have known, decided James; she was quite genuinely desperate to save Emma from finding her father dead.

James watched Margaret bend over her brother. This is pretence, he thought.

Margaret straightened up again and turned to Guy, who answered her unspoken questions.

'Emma is downstairs with her friends. I was just about to call the police when you arrived. Don't touch anything. Just look.

You too, James.'

On the low table beside the armchair was a small round tray on which stood a whisky bottle nearly empty, a tumbler containing the dregs of a pale yellow liquid, and a round plastic bottle lying empty on its side, with its lid lying beside it.

'Any message, any note?' asked Margaret.

'On the typewriter,' replied Guy. 'It's addressed to you—but don't touch it.'

'I don't see why not,' retorted Margaret, 'if it's addressed to me. Have you read it?'

'Yes,' Guy replied shortly.

'Oh well, it'll be made public property at the inquest. Do you want to come and see, James?'

She doesn't seem to be showing any signs of shock or distress, thought James as he walked over to look at the letter that Margaret held out for him to read.

'Dear Margaret,' it ran. 'I'm sorry to do this but I can't see any other way. It'll be better for Emma to have me dead than to have me tried and jailed. And I couldn't face the constant running away. And I miss Linda so badly. She'd be alive now if it hadn't been for me. Look after Emma, Margaret, please. Don't let her think too badly of me. I love her so much. I'm so sorry—so terribly sorry. Please forgive me, Meg—your wretched brother Tony.'

There were a lot of typing errors in the last

part of the letter, and underneath the typescript was an illegible scrawl.

'Is that his usual signature?' asked James.

He had to repeat the question. Margaret appeared to be hypnotised by the letter.

'Yes,' she said eventually, and for the first time sounded quite tearful. 'He's always had the most impossible handwriting.' Then, almost inaudibly, she added, 'I suppose it really is better this way. What do you think, Guy?'

'I think we ought not to delay any longer in calling the police.'

'Can't we leave it till morning? It won't make any difference to Tony. I don't want Emma to have to answer questions.'

'Emma won't have to give any evidence.' Guy spoke quite sharply. 'She hasn't been up here at all. She gave me her key and went straight to her friends when we arrived. I've been down to tell them about Tony and I came back up here to telephone.'

'Didn't she want to see her father?'

'I don't think she's really taken it in yet.'

'Then I'm going down,' said Margaret with determination. 'She's got to have a chance to see her father peacefully before the police come.'

'Do you think that's wise?'

The argument became quite heated. James, listening and wondering at Guy's vehemence, asked himself what he would do if the child was his own responsibility. After a moment's thought he spoke his answer aloud.

'Why don't you let Emma decide for herself? She's quite capable of it, and I'm sure she knows much more about her father's activities than you think.'

He very nearly added, 'and about her mother's, and about her mother's death,' but stopped himself in time.

Guy and Margaret stopped arguing and stared at him in surprise, as if they had forgotten he was there. Then Margaret said, 'You're absolutely right, James. I'll go down and ask Emma now.' And she hurried out of the room.

Guy picked up the phone.

'Can't the police wait a little longer?' said James.

'We've delayed too long already,' replied Guy, and continued with his call.

James shrugged and began to wander around the room, thinking about its owner. What had he really been like, Margaret's brother? Certainly not in the least like her. A younger brother presumably, judging from her protective attitude towards him. A weak man, easily influenced by others. But he must have been good at his job, or he would never have survived a partnership with Jack Easebourne.

James studied the bookshelves. Textbooks

222

on economics, taxation, banking, fiscal policy, etcetera. But what were his hobbies, what were his interests outside his profession? There was a shelf of paperback spy stories and crime novels. That too was predictable. And then at last something unexpected: a row of cookery books, followed by some on herbal remedies, alternative medicine, and one entitled *How to Stop Poisoning Yourself with Alcohol.*

A thought struck James. He turned to Guy, who had sat down in one of the big leather armchairs and was resting his head on his hand.

'Was your brother-in-law a teetotaller?' asked James. 'Had he been an alcoholic?'

'Yes to both questions,' replied Guy without moving his head.

'Then why the whisky? I thought they had to keep right away from it—not to have any alcohol in the house.'

'That's right,' said Guy.

'I suppose he could have got some to give him courage, or to speed up the working of the pills. Unless somebody deliberately fed it to him until he was too muddled to know what he was swallowing. What do you think, Guy? Is this whole scene faked to hide a murder?'

Guy still did not move, not even when Margaret and Emma came into the room. At the same moment the front doorbell rang, and since none of the others made any move to answer it, James went to let in the police, and found he was staring at a familiar face, tired-looking and no longer young.

'Good Lord, it's the same sergeant!' he exclaimed. 'Jones, wasn't it? Whatever are you doing here?'

'No mystery at all,' was the reply. 'It's all in my patch. This is Mr. Goff,' he said to the police constable standing beside him. 'The man who isn't Professor Leeming. We met at the Windsor Clinic this afternoon.'

'Professor Leeming is here,' said James, recovering from his surprise. 'It's his brother-in-law who's overdosed.'

They came into Tony's study to find Emma standing in front of the armchair where her father lay dead, confronting Margaret and Guy.

'I'm going to tell the police what I think,' she was saying. 'I don't believe that Dad just killed himself. Not without somebody else pushing him into it. He was much too scared of dying. I'm *sure* there was somebody else—I'm sure, I'm sure!'

'But Emma darling,' began Margaret.

The child pushed her aunt away. 'Dad didn't kill himself without encouragement,' she repeated, very calmly, without the slightest trace of hysteria.

Margaret and Guy began to protest, but Emma looked past them and appealed to James.

'Tell them he didn't,' she said. 'You know he didn't. Somebody made him do it.'

'Good evening,' said Margaret to the sergeant who was standing near the door. 'I'm afraid my niece is overwrought—the awful shock of finding her father dead, although we've been doing our best to spare her.'

Acting again, thought James, glancing at Margaret, and his suspicions of her returned yet again. She was terribly anxious about Emma, that was true, but she was also anxious not to let Emma tell her own story.

'Can we take things in order, please,' said the sergeant. 'Who found Mr. Fielding?'

'I did,' said Guy.

'And you are?'

'Professor Guy Leeming.'

The sergeant gave a quick glance at James before continuing with his questions. Several times Margaret tried to break in. The sergeant said that her turn would come, and returned to Guy's statement. After a minute or two, Emma broke away from Margaret's encircling arm; she came across to where James was perched on the arm of a chair and clung to his hand.

The questioning seemed to go on for a long time, and James began to feel very sleepy. He listened to Margaret interpreting Tony's suicide note. Yes, she had suspected for some time that her brother had been

225

handling money derived from the sale of hard drugs; she herself had challenged him with it.

No, she didn't know who else, if anyone, was involved. They would have to enquire at her brother's office. Perhaps his chief assistant, Mr. Christopher Peach, would be able to help. And yes, she knew her brother was very worried and had been very depressed since his wife's death.

She agreed that it looked from the letter as if he expected to be charged with a criminal offence, although she personally knew nothing about this. And yes, that was certainly her brother's signature at the end of the letter.

The sergeant then turned to James, who spoke very briefly, and finally to Emma.

'May I offer you my most sincere sympathy, Miss Fielding?'

Emma, still showing no sign of emotion apart from clutching at James's hand, looked up at the sergeant.

'Would you like to make a statement?' he asked.

She nodded, then asked in a very low voice, 'Please can we go to another room?'

'Certainly. This is your home. Will you show me where to go?'

Emma let go of James's hand and went to the door. The sergeant, with a sign to his colleague to remain behind, followed Emma out of the room.

Margaret took a step towards them and then, with an eloquent shrug of the shoulders, returned to her seat beside Guy and murmured something to him.

James got to his feet. 'I'd like to make a phone call,' he said to nobody in particular.

Guy looked up and inclined his head slightly to the telephone on the desk.

'I'm sure Emma wouldn't mind,' said James. 'I suppose this place belongs to her now.'

Nobody spoke. James made his call. The quiet voice of Mrs. Wimborne, the doctor's wife, answered him.

'Everything is fine, Mr. Goff. Mrs. Glenning woke up about half an hour ago and asked for some tea and biscuits. She's sleeping again now. I'll tell her you called, if she wakes.'

'Many thanks,' said James. 'I'll ring again as soon as I can.'

He sat down, and there was silence in the room until the sergeant returned. He was not accompanied by Emma.

'Miss Fielding has gone down to her friends in the basement flat,' he said. 'She is going straight to bed there and doesn't want to talk to anybody else tonight.' He turned to the constable. 'Hasn't the doctor come yet?'

The constable shook his head.

'He can't be much longer,' said the

sergeant. And then, to the others, 'That's all for tonight. We'll be in touch. We know where to get hold of you.'

'Then I'm going straight back to Sussex,' said James promptly. 'What about you two?'

'We're staying here, of course,' said Margaret. 'I take it you've no objection,' she added to the sergeant, who looked doubtful. 'This is my brother's home,' she said icily. 'For many years it has been, on and off, my home as well. My husband is exhausted and so am I. No doubt you will want to lock up this room when you have finished your business. We shall be using the kitchen, the bathroom, and one of the bedrooms. Have you any objection to that?'

'We could go to a hotel,' said Guy wearily.

'At this hour?'

'Well, I'll be off,' said James, 'if you are quite sure you don't want me to drive you home.'

Nobody replied, but before he collected his car he went down to the basement flat. Betty opened the door.

'Emma?' he asked.

'She's all right. She and Jasmine have gone to bed. I can hear them talking, but I'm not going to disturb them. If Emma wants to stay here and talk to Jasmine, then that is what's best for her.'

'I absolutely agree. But I'm afraid her aunt won't. And I'm sure you are going to have a

228

visit from her.'

'I shall have gone to bed and locked up for the night. Don't worry, James. We'll look after Emma. And I wish we could look after you too,' she added. 'You look all in. The sofa in the living-room is quite comfortable if you'd like to have a few hours' sleep.'

'I think I will,' said James, 'if I could just make a phone call first.'

'Of course.'

The news of Paula was just the same. James thanked Mrs. Wimborne, promised to be back by nine o'clock in the morning if she could stay on till then, laid his head down on the cushions that Jasmine's mother had placed for him, and was asleep within minutes.

CHAPTER NINETEEN

'Are you sure she's going to be all right?' asked James.

'Absolutely sure,' replied Dr. Wimborne, who was standing by Paula's bed with a hand on her wrist. 'I could give her a stimulant, but it's much better to let her sleep off the sedation in her own time.'

'How long is that likely to be?'

James was very impatient. He was longing to get Paula back to London and into trustworthy care before Margaret and Guy returned home.

'I'm afraid I can't say. It might be within the next hour or two, or it might be even longer before she finally shakes it off.'

Dr. Wimborne was as calm and reassuring as his wife, who had become concerned about Paula's inability to wake up and had summoned him shortly before James arrived.

'I can't tell you any more,' he went on, 'because I don't know what she has been given.'

'Would it be by injection?'

'It could well be.'

'But why should Margaret,' began James, then broke off and said unhappily, 'I never ought to have left Paula alone, even for a quarter of an hour. I had a feeling that Margaret had already been into the house when I saw her putting her car away, but I got so caught up in her desperation to get to London at once...'

'I know,' said Mrs. Wimborne softly. 'Margaret does have that sort of effect on you. But truly there is no harm done. Paula really did need the rest, didn't she, dear?' She turned to her husband, who repeated his reassurances.

'I'm quite sure there was no intention of any harm to Mrs. Glenning. Nothing except to ensure that she remained asleep and undisturbed for twelve hours or more.'

'I'll just have to wait here then,' said James at last. 'I had hoped to get her away before Guy and Margaret got back.'

James spoke without thinking, and realising suddenly that this must sound rather odd and ungrateful to these friends of the Leemings, he hastily added, 'We've caused them quite enough trouble already at a time when they've got so many worries of their own.'

'I don't think they'll be here till this afternoon,' said Dr. Wimborne. 'When Professor Leeming phoned me he seemed to think there were to be more police enquiries this morning.'

James thanked them both, but still remained anxious. It would be nice to think that he and Paula could now remove themselves completely from the series of events that had been set in motion by Paula's interest in the next-door patient at the Windsor Clinic, but James could not believe it. They were much too personally involved. What he had said to Margaret yesterday on the way to London could not be forgotten by either of them. Somebody had made sure that Linda Fielding would not recover from her accident or suicide attempt—whichever it was—and now it looked as if somebody might have done something similar with Linda's husband.

Could the police be relied on to get to the

231

truth? Could it possibly be Margaret herself who had wished her sister-in-law and her brother dead? Or had Jack Easebourne contrived the lot? Or one of the matrons?

The questions kept boiling up in James's mind as he talked to Dr. and Mrs. Wimborne.

'When she wakes up properly,' he asked, 'what shall I give Paula?'

'Tea, coffee, something to eat—anything she fancies. She'll probably be rather sleepy the rest of the day, but she'll be fit for the drive. If you're in any doubt, give me a ring.'

It was a relief when they went at last, these kind and trustworthy people. But on the other hand the frustration was almost intolerable. To be alone with Paula at last, free to talk, to share ideas and try to come to some conclusions, yet unable to take advantage of the opportunity, was so frustrating that James hardly knew how to get through the hours.

He tried to concentrate on practical little details. Must remember to leave Guy's keys somewhere for Guy to find them. Might as well tidy the kitchen and wash the cups and plates that had been used. Yet another mug of coffee now. Any whisky anywhere? No. Don't really want it.

Whisky. So Tony had been an alcoholic and had managed to conquer it. With whose help? His wife's? Jack's, Margaret's? They

232

must all have known about it, must have realised his vulnerability.

And Emma. She must have known too.

Emma. That was another positive action he could take.

James picked up the telephone in the sitting-room, where he had been pacing restlessly up and down. When he had come away from Betty's basement flat, after a few hours' sleep, he had left both the girls and Jasmine's mother fast asleep.

Betty answered the call. Yes, Emma was all right. Very shocked and distressed of course, but fairly calm. She seemed to want to be with Jasmine all the time, and Betty thought that was best for them. She herself was not going to work today, and she was keeping Jasmine off school. The police sergeant had been in again and had talked privately to Emma for quite a long time. She—Betty—was impressed by the way he dealt with the child. It had raised her opinion of the police, which had not been very high up till now.

As to the Leemings, well, Margaret had been down of course; Betty had talked to her on the entry-phone but refused to let her in, saying Emma was still sleeping and was not to be disturbed. Whether she could keep this up indefinitely, especially if Professor Leeming were to intervene for his wife, Betty did not know. After all, Margaret was

233

Emma's nearest relative now, and would generally be regarded as her rightful guardian. If there was a combined assault by both the Leemings—

'I should let Emma deal with it herself,' said James. 'She's perfectly capable of it. But please keep me informed.'

The call came to an end, and yet again James went upstairs to look at Paula, felt a little surge of hope when she seemed to be stirring, and sighed deeply when she sank back into peaceful sleep.

'You could shake her and pour coffee into her,' Dr. Wimborne had said, 'but she's had so much stress that it's much better to let her take her time.'

So what do I do next, James asked himself as he came downstairs again. Browsing round Guy's library took up another half hour, and then he returned to Paula and began to talk to her aloud, as if she were listening.

'Do hurry up, darling, I've got such a lot to say ... I've got an idea I want to discuss with you. You may think it crazy, but...'

The monologue was interrupted by the phone ringing in the room next door, which was Margaret's. This was the first time he had entered it, and he glanced round as he went to answer the call. Divan bed, couple of chairs, large table, plenty of bookshelves, and an old roll-top desk that James decided to investigate as soon as the call was over.

He had no qualms about snooping; he was only rather surprised that he had not thought of coming in here before.

'Yes?' he said into the mouthpiece.

'Is that you, James?' Margaret's voice, very cool and businesslike. 'How's Paula?'

'Dr. Wimborne says she'll be all right, but he's rather curious to know what drug you gave her. Personally I'm even more interested in your motive.'

A short pause the other end of the line, and then Margaret said, 'I hardly expect you to believe me, but it really was a nursing decision. Paula isn't yet fit for so much activity and badly needs rest. I'll explain to Dr. Wimborne myself when I see him.'

'What time are you coming?'

'This afternoon. We've got a lot to attend to here.'

'Margaret, tell me straight. Did you expect to find Tony dead?'

'I thought it possible. In fact, very likely.'

'Why?'

'I can't tell you.'

'Were you with him before he died?'

'No.'

'Had you spoken to him on the phone?'

'Yes,' replied Margaret, 'and I'm not answering any more questions on the phone now. I'll tell you all I can later on. I'm only calling to ask about Paula and to say that

235

there'll be a parcel of books arriving for Guy this morning and there may be something to pay on them. So if you wouldn't mind—'

'Of course I will. Any other household instructions?'

'Only to help yourself to anything you want. Shall we see you when we get back?'

'It depends on Paula. Dr. Wimborne says I can bring her up to London when she wakes up properly.'

'Where are you taking her?'

'I'd rather not tell you.'

'All right. So we don't trust each other. Point taken. No need to labour it, James.'

'I'm sorry, Margaret. And I'm truly sorry about your brother.'

'Thank you. I wondered if you were ever going to say that. Guy's calling me—I'll have to go now.'

'Hold on a minute,' said James, 'I wanted to ask—how's Emma?'

'Almost as suspicious of me as you are yourself,' said Margaret bitterly. 'I've got to go.'

She rang off, leaving James feeling sorry for her and guilty about his own behaviour, but still determined to have a look inside the roll-top desk. The simple mechanism had always fascinated him. As he pushed back the cover he could remember as a young child going into his grandfather's study, which was strictly forbidden territory, and

236

playing with his desk.

So vivid was the recollection that for a moment James half expected to see sheets of paper covered in G. E. Goff's neat small handwriting lying there, and he was almost surprised to find himself reading an estimate from a landscape gardening firm about extending a beech hedge.

Further investigation revealed documents relating to other domestic matters— electricity bills, insurances, a folder labelled 'Car.' Even in the pigeon-holes James could find no trace of the sort of private correspondence he was looking for. An envelope labelled 'Letters to be answered' held only a couple of postcards and a scrap of paper on which was written, 'Send May recipe for carrot cake.'

James felt torn between exasperation and amusement. All he had discovered was that Margaret looked after everything to do with the house and garden and car, and that either she had very little personal correspondence or else never kept any letters.

There remained only one pigeon-hole to explore. If this yielded nothing then he would have to give up, because the drawers of the desk were all locked and James could see no hope of finding any keys.

From the last pigeon-hole—a very narrow one—James extracted two passports. Guy's and Margaret's, he said to himself, but in fact they were both Margaret's. Presumably Guy's, recently used, was among his possessions downstairs. He opened Margaret's latest passport, uncovering a typically unflattering photograph and the fact that she was born in Bogotá fifty years ago.

Older than he had expected. Was there anything to be made of the South American connection? Drugs sprang to mind instantly. James flicked through the pages of the passport, telling himself that he was doing what he so often accused Paula of doing—letting the imagination roam too freely.

He picked up the old passport, with the top right-hand corner of the cover snipped off. Why had she kept it? The answer came quickly: because it contained a U.S. visa which was still valid, and it was less trouble to travel with both documents than to get the visa transferred from one to the other.

James was just about to replace the two passports when a piece of paper fell out of the earlier one. Not particularly hopeful, and assuming it was some piece of bureaucratic information, James picked it up.

But it was in handwriting, an illegible scrawl, and it looked like a prescription. At the top was printed 'J. L. Easebourne,' followed by a long string of degrees and qualifications and an address in North London, and at the bottom was a barely distinguishable note, 'Repeat if necessary.'

James stood and stared, convinced that he had come across something very important. Tucked into the back of an old passport—not a bad hiding place. Could he make a copy of the prescription? He didn't think so. Dare he take it away?

He was debating whether to do so when the front doorbell rang loudly, shocking him into a further paralysis of uncertainty—then he remembered that Guy and Margaret would hardly be likely to ring their own front doorbell.

Hastily he put the slip of paper into his jacket pocket, replaced the passports, glanced round to check that everything looked as he had found it, and pulled down the lid of the desk.

The bell rang again as he ran downstairs, and when he opened the door an impatient young man snapped, 'Two pounds to pay,' thrust a heavy parcel at him, grabbed the money from James, and returned to his van without another word.

James dumped the parcel on Guy's desk, went to the kitchen and made two cups of instant coffee, and carried them up to Paula's room. Whatever Dr. Wimborne said, he was going to wake her up thoroughly now. It turned out to be not as difficult as he had feared. Paula drank all the coffee and smiled at him. 'Sorry, love, for being so useless,' she murmured. 'I feel as if I could sleep for ever. What's the time? What's happening?'

'It's nearly midday and we're going to London. You're booked into a little convalescent home suggested by Louise. It's very near both your flat and mine, and you can come and go as much as you feel fit for. Come on. Get some clothes on. The sooner we're out of this place the better.'

Yawning and blinking, Paula allowed herself to be made ready for travel. A third cup of strong coffee restored her to something more approaching her normal alert self, and for the first half hour of the journey she actually listened to James's answers to her questions and gave it as her opinion that Tony really had killed himself, but that somebody—most likely Jack—had provided the means. After that she dozed on and off. Several times James found that he had been talking to himself, but once, when he had thought Paula wasn't listening, she said, 'Did you know that Margaret provides most of the money and that the house actually belongs to her?'

'How do you know that?'

'Something Guy said when we were talking about his first wife. Margaret nursed her till she died of cancer. Guy almost bankrupted himself to make sure she had the best of everything.'

'You don't mean Guy married Margaret for her money?'

'Not exactly, but he likes to be made comfortable.'

'And why did she marry him?' asked James.

'For status. To spite Jack, show him that she didn't care that he'd finished with her and had switched to Linda Fielding.'

'Ah,' said James, 'so you'd come to that conclusion too.'

'I was trying to tell you when I kept falling asleep. It's terribly frustrating not to be able to investigate anything myself.'

'Never mind, darling. You lie in bed and exercise the little grey cells. And talk to Louise, of course.'

'Is she going to be there?'

'Some of the time. She knows the matron and she does an occasional night duty.'

With great relief James transferred Paula to the care of Louise and her friend. Louise came back to his car with him, and James passed on the comments of Dr. Wimborne and his wife.

'You know that Tony Fielding is dead?' he added.

'Who doesn't? The Windsor Clinic is buzzing with it. Police enquiries and all this morning. But it's nothing compared with the excitements of this afternoon.'

'Why—what's happened?' asked James.

'The big white chief himself. Jack Easebourne.'

'What's he done? Do hurry up, Louise. I want you to get back to Paula.'

'He's disappeared. Cancelled all his rounds without giving any reason and got Miss Twigg to see his patients. And that's not all. Somebody else has disappeared as well.'

'Let me guess. Not your Matron—no. The Heath House glamour girl—Rachel Feverel. Am I right?'

'Perfectly right. I was afraid you were going to say Margaret Leeming.'

'Oh no,' said James. 'That's not the part Margaret's been playing. Far from it. Don't worry, Louise. I was rather fascinated by the lady for a little while. Still am, as a matter of fact, but not in that way. You go and look after Paula now. I've got some more enquiries to make.'

'Windsor Clinic?'

'Eventually. But somewhere else first.'

'Where? Who?'

'Tell you later.'

Louise tried to ask him again, but James got into his car, waved, and drove away.

CHAPTER TWENTY

Jasmine's mother came to the door of the basement flat.

'How's Emma?' asked James.

'She's up and down. I was really worried about her when Sergeant Jones came back this morning, but Emma was determined to talk to him, and she seemed to calm down a little after he left.'

'What did she tell him, Betty?'

'It must be something about her father's death—and her mother's too, I suspect, but beyond that I've no idea.'

'Do you think Jasmine knows?'

'She must know, but she won't say a word if Emma doesn't want her to. I don't like it. It's not right for the children to be burdened like this.'

She sat down at the big table in the living-room and James did likewise.

'I don't like it either,' he said, 'but I suppose it's better for Emma to talk about it than to bottle it up. Whatever it is that she knows,' he added.

'I suppose so,' sighed Betty. 'And Jasmine has already had to learn that life can be very tough.'

James did not reply, and for a minute or two they sat in thoughtful silence. Then

243

James said, 'Where are they now?'

'The children? Upstairs.'

'Oh. Are Margaret and Guy still there?'

'No. They went an hour or more ago. Very upset that Emma refused to go with them. I've got to confess, James, that I rather wish she had gone with them. She's got to get used to the fact that her home will have to be with them until she's old enough to make one for herself.'

'True enough,' said James without enthusiasm, then added, 'I'd like to talk to Emma. I'll go up and send Jasmine home, shall I?'

'Yes, please. Then she can get on with her project. School term ends next week and she'll never get it finished with all these interruptions.'

It was the dark girl, Jasmine, who opened the door of Tony's flat to James. She looked tired and strained, he thought, and he could understand her mother's worry.

'Is Emma here?' he asked.

'Yes,' she said shortly.

'Would she talk to me, do you think?'

'I'll go and ask her,' replied Jasmine. 'She's looking at some of her dad's papers at the moment.'

'Haven't the police taken them away, or locked them up?'

'Emma says the sergeant suggested she should,' said Jasmine. 'Please wait here while

244

I ask her.'

Just like a housemaid, thought James, or a private secretary; and he could understand even more her mother's concern.

But Jasmine herself did not seem to resent Emma's domination. In fact James suspected that some part of her was even rather enjoying her role when she came back and announced that Emma had finished.

'That's fine,' said James. 'How about you going home now? I think your mother wants you.'

'Okay,' said Jasmine, and ran off humming to herself and looking like a twelve-year-old girl again.

Emma, too, looked so young and pale that James felt great pity and longed to comfort her. She was sitting at her father's desk and holding in both hands a sealed envelope.

'I think this is what the sergeant wanted to give to his inspector,' she said, looking up as James came into the room. 'It's a sort of agreement between my father and Mr. Easebourne. Auntie Margaret and I found it when we were looking for a photograph of my mother.'

James pulled up a chair and sat beside her. 'Are the police going to make your father's activities public?' he asked.

'Sergeant Jones hopes it won't be necessary,' replied Emma. 'He thinks the note will probably be enough for them to bring in a verdict of suicide at the inquest, but he wants more evidence against Mr. Easebourne. So do I. I wish it could be proved that he killed my Dad. That's what I'm trying to find.'

'I see,' said James softly. 'Did you talk about it to the sergeant?'

'Yes. He was very interested and he says it's quite likely that Mr. Easebourne was partly responsible, but he doesn't think it's going to be possible to prove anything.'

Emma had been speaking quite calmly, but as she finished her voice rose and she got up and stamped her foot in fury and cried out, glancing at James, 'He killed my mother and he's driven my father to death and they can't do anything, anything at all!'

James neither moved nor spoke. There's nothing at all one can do or say to make her feel better, he said to himself. But she knows I'm here, she knows I'm with her all the way.

Emma stamped her foot again, then returned to her seat at the desk and said, 'I always wanted to sit here when I was very young. Dad used to let me sometimes as a treat, and he'd stand in front of me and say, "And what are your orders for today, madam?"'

James got up and stood in front of the desk.

'Well, what are they?' he said. 'Tell me what you want done and I'll do my best to carry it out.'

'You don't mean it,' said Emma. 'You'll only go so far, like Sergeant Jones, and then say there's no proof.'

'I'm not interested in proof, only in the truth.'

'Are you?' She regarded him thoughtfully. 'Paula is, I know. But Paula's not well enough.'

'But I'm well enough. What's all this about Mr. Easebourne killing your mother?'

'They were lovers.' Emma looked up at him angrily. 'Don't laugh at me, don't say I'm too young to understand. Of course I knew. I knew all the time when my mother was supposed to be going for treatment and Auntie Margaret came to look after me and pretended and pretended.'

'I'm not laughing and I'm not saying you're too young,' said James, sitting down again. 'And I'd actually come to the same conclusion myself about your mother and Jack Easebourne. May I go on with my theory? Don't bother to say anything if I'm right—just interrupt me if I've got it wrong.'

Emma, who had buried her face in her hands, gave a slight nod.

'What I would guess,' went on James, 'is that it used to be Mr. Easebourne and your Aunt Margaret, and then he got to know your mother and switched to her, but she felt miserable and guilty all the time because of you and your father. And she couldn't see any way out of her difficulties, and she really loved you and your father, and thought you'd be better without her, and she took an overdose of drugs, but it wasn't enough to kill her, and she was taken to the Windsor Clinic for treatment to bring her round, but in spite of that, she died. Various people expressed surprise, because she ought to have recovered with the proper treatment, but nobody was blamed because there was no proof.'

Emma raised her head and stared at him. Her eyes were misted and her cheeks were very flushed. 'You're right so far,' she said. 'Go on.'

'The next bit is very much guesswork,' said James. 'I think both you and your father suspected that your mother had been given the wrong treatment at the Windsor, very likely on purpose, but you and your father never talked about it. It was just too painful to be mentioned between you. You were both so desolate after her death that you had to support each other, and the only way to keep going was to keep quiet and pretend. Dear Emma.'

James stretched out a hand to touch the girl's arm; she had once more hidden her face in her hands.

'I think you did quite right, both of you,' continued James. 'Some wounds are best

248

just covered up and left to heal as much as they can. But I would guess that there was one person who didn't want it completely covered up, and that was your Aunt Margaret. Do you believe it was she who actually let your mother die?'

Emma shook her head violently.

'Then who was it?'

'He did,' muttered Emma.

'Jack Easebourne. Why do you think so?'

'Because Mummy was a nuisance to him. He couldn't trust her.'

'Do you think he himself actually gave her a fatal dose, or withdrew the treatment that would have saved her, or do you think he got somebody at the clinic to do it for him?'

'It's the same thing, isn't it?' said Emma, looking up at James.

'Not quite. If he had an accomplice, that person will suffer severe penalties if the whole business is brought out into the open and the crime can be proved.'

'I suppose so,' said Emma without much interest.

So she doesn't think the accomplice was her Aunt Margaret, thought James. Then what is the cause of her antipathy towards Margaret?

He asked the question aloud. Emma replied, 'She could help me but she won't. She knows Mr. Easebourne killed my mum and she knows what he did to my father and she won't say, she won't say!'

As she spoke, Emma banged her hand hard on the desk, gave a little squeal of pain, and raised the other hand to soothe it.

'Why do you think she won't say?' asked James. 'Do you think she is still in love with him and wants to protect him?'

'I don't know,' muttered Emma, still nursing her hand.

But I do know, said James to himself. Margaret has been protecting Jack because she's blackmailing him. The last thing a blackmailer wants is for the victim's misdeeds to be made public. But if Jack really has run away, then the whole situation will change. Shall I tell Emma that? Yes, I think I will. I've promised her the truth.

'Listen,' he said aloud, 'I heard a rumour just before I came here. At least I thought it was only a rumour but it may be true. It's that Mr. Easebourne has cancelled all his appointments and left his home and gone off with Rachel Feverel from Heath House.'

'Oh.' Emma looked completely taken aback, then disappointed. 'Does that mean he's going to get away?'

'I doubt it. If the police are on the trail of the drugs business they won't give up so easily.'

And I've got that prescription to produce, added James to himself, which must be pretty damning for Jack or else Margaret

250

wouldn't have got hold of it and be holding on to it, but I don't think I'll tell Emma about that. Let's wait until the right moment.

Emma was speaking again. 'He's going to get away, and that woman too. Why didn't she warn my father? He trusted her, he was taking refuge with her. They fixed it between them—that's how it was! They pretended Dad had to come to London to talk about an emergency, and Mr. Easebourne came here with the whisky and the pills and told Dad he was going to be arrested.'

'No proof,' said James.

Emma glared at him. 'You're as bad as Sergeant Jones. We've got to find proof!' She banged her hand on the desk again, rather more carefully this time.

'Okay,' he said, deciding that this discussion was doing her more good than a violent attack of weeping would have done. 'How do we set about it? And where does Margaret come into all this? Did she help to drive your father to suicide?'

'No, no,' cried Emma impatiently. 'She was always nagging at Dad but she loved him. She'd have saved him if she could.'

'So what was she doing last night?'

'I expect Mr. Easebourne left Dad with the whisky and the pills and Dad phoned Auntie for advice—he's no good at making decisions except at work—and she said she'd come and see him, but she came too late.'

'And found him dead. Why didn't she call the police?'

'Because she didn't want anyone to know she'd been here. And she'd be worrying about me, thinking I was still at Heath House and she'd have to come and tell me. But of course I wasn't there.'

'She was desperate to get to London when she found you'd come here with Guy,' said James. 'I believe she really did want to spare you from finding your father dead without her being there to support you. I think you're being rather unkind about your aunt, Emma.'

The child wriggled impatiently. 'I suppose I ought to go and stay with her,' she said. 'Jasmine's mum won't want me here with them for ever and I don't suppose I'll be allowed to live here at home by myself.'

'I'm afraid not,' said James, standing up. 'Come on. I've got some more enquiries to make. I'll come back later and tell you the results. Why don't you go and help Jasmine with her school project? Incidentally,' he added as they reached the door of the room, 'Oughtn't you to be at school yourself?'

'Dad told them I'd be away until the end of term. That's next week.'

'So you'll be having summer holidays, and I hereby invite you to come and stay with Paula and myself for at least part of them.

You and I will go wind-surfing while Paula lies in a beach chair watching us and going green with envy. Would you like that, Emma?'

The answer was the long held-back flood of tears and a plea to be left alone in her father's room for a while.

'Okay,' said James. 'We'll fix up holiday dates as soon as Paula is well enough, and I'll go and tell Jasmine you'll be with her in half an hour or so. 'Bye for now, Emma.'

And if Paula doesn't like it, he said to himself as he ran down the steps to the basement flat, then Emma and I will go on holiday by ourselves.

CHAPTER TWENTY-ONE

'It's Mr. Goff, isn't it?' said the girl at the reception desk.

James, so impatient to get to the matron at the Windsor Clinic that he was walking past the desk, stopped and glanced back.

'That's right,' he said. 'I have to see Mrs. Kennedy very urgently. Is she in her office?"

'No, she's gone off duty and she's not to be disturbed. Would you like to see her assistant?'

James shook his head. 'No, I've got to see Mrs. Kennedy herself. Could you tell her

I'm here. No, wait a minute,' he interrupted himself, 'if I write her a note, could you take it to her?'

The girl looked doubtful. 'I don't think we ought to. She's not well.'

James had been looking at her more closely as they talked. 'I've got it!' he exclaimed suddenly. 'You're Geraldine, aren't you? Weren't you on duty when they called the police in about me and I walked straight into the trap?'

'That's right,' she said. 'But it's nothing to the excitements we've been having today.'

'Police again?'

'Among other things. And consultants disappearing. Rumour running rife.'

'So I've heard. Tell me.'

I ought to have stopped to gossip first, said James to himself, but let's hope it's not too late to remedy that.

In fact it turned out that Geraldine had nothing of substance to tell. It was common knowledge at the Windsor Clinic that Mrs. Kennedy wanted to marry Mr. Easebourne, so naturally her very bad headache was attributed to disappointment.

James asked about the police enquiries and was told that they were in connection with the suicide of Mr. Fielding, who was of course known at the clinic as a friend of Mr. Easebourne's; that was when they discovered that the surgeon was nowhere to be found,

254

and that was when Mrs. Kennedy started getting her headache.

James listened, beginning to feel sorry for Jenny Kennedy, especially since what he had to say to her was hardly likely to ease her head. Then, when he judged the right moment had come, he asked again whether somebody could take a note from him to Matron's flat.

'It's to do with Mr. Easebourne,' he added. 'I really do think she will be willing to see me.'

Geraldine, called on to answer an enquiry from one of the nurses, pushed a memo pad and a pen towards James, who hastily wrote a couple of sentences, found an envelope on the desk, addressed and sealed it, and waited while Geraldine finished talking to the nurse.

'Hi, Sarah,' she called out as the latter was turning away. 'You're going upstairs. Could you ring Matron's bell and drop this through the letter-box? Thanks a lot.'

Three minutes later James achieved his object. Mrs. Kennedy, out of uniform and in a pleasant little sitting-room full of photographs and small china animals, looked unhappy, vulnerable, and oddly enough rather younger than she did when on duty.

'I'm truly sorry to bother you at this moment,' said James, 'but it's got to come sooner or later and I thought you might be glad to get it over.'

Her answer was to offer him a cigarette. He shook his head and she put the box away. James pulled out of his wallet the piece of paper that had fallen out of Margaret's old passport and showed it to Mrs. Kennedy.

'Of course I can't make any sense of this,' he said, 'but am I right in thinking it was used to hasten Linda Fielding's death, and maybe that of others already weakened by illness or by drugs?'

She stared at the prescription and James, watching her closely, thought he could read both alarm and relief in her face.

'Where did you get it from?' she asked.

'Can't you guess? Haven't you and Mr. Easebourne been trying for a long time to get it back from her?'

Mrs. Kennedy inclined her head. 'But why did she give it to you?'

'I can't answer that. It's between Margaret Leeming and myself. But I very much doubt that there'll be any more risk to you from that quarter.'

'She'd get nothing out of me,' said Mrs. Kennedy with a little burst of energy. 'I've got no money nor anything else to offer her. What are you going to do with that prescription?'

'That depends on you. Would you be willing to give evidence in court against Jack?'

There was a silence while Mrs. Kennedy

stared down at her hands, lying idle in her lap. James was rather surprised by her stillness; then he realised that it was the lethargy of one who could see nothing to hope for.

'What is it to you?' she asked at last.

'I'm thinking of a child who is in much the same position as yourself,' he replied. 'She has lost everything she cared for and cannot at the moment see how she can face the future.'

'The Fieldings' little girl,' said Mrs. Kennedy without looking up.

'Yes,' said James. 'I think it would help her to have the truth brought out and the man brought to justice. It might help you too,' he added after a moment's pause, 'to clear the past away and make a completely fresh start.'

'A fresh start with a prison sentence?'

As she spoke, she looked up at him at last and smiled bitterly.

'I don't see why it should come to that if you prove you were simply carrying out doctor's orders. Am I right in assuming that this stuff'—he touched the piece of paper—'is only fatal if taken by somebody already drugged?'

'Yes, that's right,' she said.

'What would it be used for normally and legitimately?'

'As a strong sedative.'

'That should let you out then. I'll gladly help with your defence,' he added, 'if it should come to that, but I don't believe it will.'

There was a long silence. Then the matron said, 'What do you want me to do?'

'Help the police to trace Jack. They're already on to him because of the drugs business. Tell them you think he's run away partly because of that and partly because he doesn't want to face too close an enquiry into the deaths of Mr. and Mrs. Fielding. Tell them you've come to the conclusion that Mrs. Fielding was wrongly treated, and produce this prescription.'

'And if I'm asked why I've done nothing about it up till now?'

'It's not your place to question the instructions of eminent medical men or women. And it's the suicide and the running away that reawakened your suspicions.'

There was another silence.

'All right. I'll do it,' said Mrs. Kennedy at last. 'You'd better give me that prescription. It should have been filed away with the others. I don't know how Nurse Fielding got hold of it.'

It took James a moment or two to identify 'Nurse Fielding' with Mrs. Margaret Leeming. Then he handed over the little sheet of paper.

'How do you know I'm not going to

258

destroy this the moment you've gone?' asked Mrs. Kennedy.

'It's up to you,' replied James. 'If you want Jack to get away scot-free, then go ahead.'

She made no response, and he felt that he had struck a wrong note.

'I'm sorry,' he said. 'That implies that you would act only out of vengeance, and not out of sympathy with an ill-used child.'

'Thank you,' said the matron with a hint of irony. Then she got to her feet. 'Would you like some coffee? Tea? Sherry?'

James stood up. 'No thanks. I've got some more calls to make this evening.'

'Margaret Leeming?'

'Probably.'

'And what, I wonder, will that be about,' said Mrs. Kennedy. She looked more relaxed, thought James, than when he had arrived. She even sounded genuinely amused.

'You have something to ask her, no doubt,' she went on. 'Will it be a threat or an appeal?'

'You know her well,' said James as they moved towards the door. 'What approach do you advise?'

'I don't think you need any lessons at all in the art of moral or emotional blackmail,' she replied, 'but it's as well to remember, with Margaret Leeming, that she's very unreliable because she's always acting.'

'Always? I should have thought that in her work at any rate she was genuine—a devoted nurse.'

'When she has a motive, she can play that part as well as any other.'

'I see,' said James. 'By the way, would you say that she suffers from paranoia?'

The matron thought for a moment. 'Sometimes,' she replied. 'She has bouts of acute depression—that's when her acting fails her—and she is convinced that everybody is against her.'

'I see,' said James again. 'Then quite apart from being a blackmailer, you would not say that she was a suitable person to be in charge of the upbringing of an orphaned child?'

'Definitely not.'

'Would you be willing to take an oath on that if need be?'

'You're asking a lot, aren't you?' Again Mrs. Kennedy sounded mildly amused. 'What do I get out of all this—a clear conscience, the chance to make a fresh start?'

'You've said it,' said James. 'May I keep in touch? If there's any way in which I could be of any use to you—I really mean that, you know.'

'I know you do. Goodbye.'

Downstairs, Geraldine at the reception desk was obviously expecting another gossip. 'How did you find Matron?' she asked.

'I think she's feeling a bit better now,' replied James. 'She's been having rather a bad time, poor soul. Thanks for all your help. 'Bye, Geraldine.'

Outside, opening the door of his car, he wondered where to go next. He had promised to report progress to Emma, he wanted to go and see Paula, and to complete the tasks he had set himself he ought to go down to Sussex to see Margaret.

But as he drove away from the Windsor Clinic he became more and more reluctant to do any of these things. His own apartment was only minutes away. He became suddenly very conscious that the day had become hot and sultry, that he was tired of talking to people, and that the only thing he really wanted to do was to make a pot of his own favourite brand of tea, settle down in his favourite armchair, and stroke Rosie and listen to her purring.

After an hour of carrying out this programme, James began to revive a little. There was still time to drive down to Sussex this evening, but he was very reluctant to do so. Couldn't he do it by phone?

'Margaret—I want to look after Emma. Be her legal guardian if possible, but in any case have the final say in how and where she is to live and go to school. If you don't agree, then I've got the evidence of your own blackmailing activities and I shan't hesitate

261

to use it.'

Could one say that over the phone? Or would it be better to write it?

No. Nothing in writing. It would have to be by phone, because he didn't want to see her again. He couldn't tell how she was going to react. It might be very easy or she might decide to fight, but he knew he was going to win in the end. As Jenny Kennedy had said, he didn't need any lessons in the art of moral blackmail.

And after working on Margaret, he thought, as he got up and went into the kitchen to give Rosie her dinner, he might have to exercise this talent once again. There had been no opportunity to discuss his plans for Emma with Paula. Events had moved too fast for that. It was strange that he wasn't quite sure how Paula would take it.

'She's so terribly cautious at heart,' he said to Rosie as he put her bowl of pilchards down on the floor. 'I'm the impulsive one. Like when I adopted you.'

Rosie licked his finger before settling down to eat.

'You were a deserted and starving cat, but Paula was quite surprised when she found I was going to keep you. But later on she was quite envious and wished she'd given you a home herself. It'll be the same with Emma. At least I hope so. And if it isn't...'

James straightened up and began to

prepare himself a meal. If it isn't, he said to himself as he sat down at the kitchen table to eat his omelette, then I shall just go ahead with my plans and let Paula and Emma sort it out between the two of them.